'You don't hav
Abbey. I a

Her reply was ... words. 'But not ... ou is a waste of time.'

Rohan put his han... her shoulder. 'I'm going to stay on for a while.'

Abbey turned her head to look at him, unable to believe what he'd just said. 'Why would you decide to stay in Gladstone?'

He smoothed her cheek. 'Why do you think?'

This was too important, and she didn't want to look like a fool. 'I don't have the energy for games, Rohan. Suppose you tell me.'

'Until they catch this person who's been harassing you and your family, I can't leave. I'd never rest, not knowing that you were all safe.'

Abbey choked back the bitter disappointment. Rohan was a good friend but he was never going to be more than that.

The next problem would be when he did leave. She was frightened now that she'd admitted she'd fallen in love with him.

MARRIAGE AND MATERNITY

**Dedicated midwives, devoted sisters—
it's time for the Wilson sisters to find the courage
for marriage—and a family of their own!**

For Abbey, Bella and Kirsten Wilson
marriage and midwifery just don't mix.

Balancing work and home life isn't on their agenda,
because caring for each other and delivering babies
to the women of Gladstone New South Wales
is a full-time occupation.

It will take three very special men to persuade these
three remarkable and dedicated women that they
deserve marriage—and babies too.

MIDWIFE IN NEED

Midwife Abbey Wilson has spent her life
caring for everyone but herself. Rohan Roberts—
the new doctor at Gladstone Maternity—is determined
to show her what her own needs really are!

Look out for Bella's and Kirsten's stories
coming in 2004 from
Mills & Boon® Medical Romance™!

MIDWIFE IN NEED

BY
FIONA McARTHUR

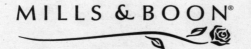

MILLS & BOON®

First published in Great Britain 2003
Harlequin Mills & Boon Limited,
Eton House, 18-24 Paradise Road, Richmond, Surrey TW9 1SR

© Fiona McArthur 2003

ISBN 0 263 83471 9

Set in Times Roman 10½ on 12½ pt.
03-0903-42857

Printed and bound in Spain
by Litografía Rosés, S.A., Barcelona

CHAPTER ONE

'THE new doctor is on his way.' Michelle put the phone down and moved around the bed to hold the young woman's hand. 'He's stuck at the railway crossing. Should be here in five.'

Abbey Wilson, Nursing Unit Manager of Gladstone Maternity, on the mid-north coast of New South Wales, nodded and sighed. They didn't require a doctor's presence for uncomplicated births, but this baby had shown signs of distress late in labour. The last gush of amniotic fluid had been thick green meconium liquor. Why did Scott have to have a sudden trip to Sydney when she needed him?

Apparently, the new doctor travelled Australia filling in as locum for general practitioners in small country towns. He'd done his anaesthetic training and also his Diploma of Obstetrics with Scott in England, so Abbey could hope he'd be competent.

'They say boy babies are more stubborn than girls—but I am *never* doing this again,' panted Vivie.

Abbey smiled across at the young woman. How many times had she heard a woman in labour promise never to return?

'You're incredible, Vivie. Hang in there, just a few moments to go,' Abbey said. 'You still need to push because your baby's head is a tight fit down here. We may have to take him over to the trolley to give some oxygen, but we'll get him back to you as soon as we can, OK?'

Vivie nodded that she understood and then she groaned.

Suddenly the baby's head started to move as Vivie pushed with the next contraction. With aching slowness his little crinkled forehead lengthened, and then with a rush his nose and lips were released from the birth canal.

'OK. Well done, Vivie.' Abbey slipped her finger in beside the baby's head and sure enough a loose loop of cord was coiled around his neck. The pulsating coil didn't have enough stretch to slip over baby's head and wasn't tight enough to warrant cutting prior to birth, so Abbey let it be.

As if by magic, Vivie's baby's head swivelled like the hands of a clock travelling from six to nine, and inside Vivie's pelvis his neck untwisted to allow his shoulders to slip under her pubic arch.

Two minutes seemed to take for ever as they waited for the next contraction which would allow the rest of him to be born. Abbey had suctioned his mouth to remove any meconium that would otherwise be drawn into the lungs at his first breath, and waited. The bluish hue of his little face darkened and Abbey resisted the impulse to encourage Vivie to push without a contraction. In nature's time, she reminded herself.

Finally, Vivie's uterus hardened with the next contraction and she groaned again. Her son's anterior shoulder dipped down then rose from the birth canal and Abbey gently supported his head as the rest of his body was born. Limp and pale, the baby lay on the bed between Vivie's legs. Abbey uncoiled the cord around his neck and another loop coiled around his arm. His cord pulse was strong and above a hundred beats a minute but he made no attempt to breathe. He was stunned by his passage through the birth canal.

Abbey quickly clamped and cut the connection between Vivie and her son and Michelle leant over and lifted the baby up for Vivie to announce the sex.

'The ultrasound was right. It is a boy,' Vivie gasped as she leaned back against the bean bag.

Abbey glanced at Vivie as Michelle carried the baby over to the resuscitaire. 'He needs some oxygen, Vivie. Michelle and I are going to dry him and use the mask. I'll have to leave you for a moment.'

'OK.' Vivie's voice was faint with relief that the birth was over. She closed her eyes.

Vivie's son lay on the resuscitaire like a pale rag doll, and when Abbey wiped him with a warm cloth, he jiggled flaccidly as the fabric moved over his skin. Dark blue eyes stared, open and unblinking, as Abbey wiped his face. She suctioned his nose and mouth again before gently placing the oxygen mask over his nose and chin while Michelle listened with the stethoscope to his heart rate.

Michelle nodded. 'One hundred and ten.'

'OK. He doesn't need any cardiac help. But he still doesn't want to take a breath.' Abbey tilted the baby's head into the sniffing position, compressed the green bag of the oxy-viva and watched his chest rise. The air pressure would encourage the inflation of his fluid-filled alveoli into working order. She started with three larger puffs, then settled into a rhythm of one small inflation of the bag per second.

When one minute had passed since birth, Abbey stopped her compressions of the bag and Michelle listened again.

'Still one hundred and ten.'

'We'll give him a two for heart rate and he gets a zero for respiratory effort.' Abbey hated it when they did that, but consoled herself with the fact that his skin was pink from the oxygen pumping around his body. They continued with the respiratory resuscitation.

A firm knock tattooed on the hallway door. A broad-shouldered stranger in a cowboy hat and linen shirt entered the birthing suite and strode across to Abbey and the baby.

'I'm Dr Roberts, I'm filling in for Scott Rainford,' he said, and tossed his hat towards the corner of the room. Abbey blinked as the black Akubra sailed through the air to settle gently on the chair. The sight was so bizarre that for a split second she had trouble marshalling her thoughts.

That was what he looked like—a marshal or sheriff

in a cowboy movie. Or maybe the cynical gunslinger? Her mind clicked back into gear. 'Dr Roberts.
Thank you for coming.' She looked away from him
to the timer on the resuscitation trolley.

'Baby is two minutes old. Heart rate above a hundred beats a minute since birth but no respiratory effort. No maternal narcotic pain relief in labour and
prior to late second stage foetal heart sounds were
stable at one hundred and twenty to one-thirty beats
a minute. His umbilical cord was loosely around his
neck once and around his arm at birth. Good circu-
lation has improved his peripheral colour from very
pale to pink, as you see.' Abbey looked up into the
doctor's face for response and he nodded. 'If you
would like to take over the bagging, I'll leave you
with Nurse while I check on Vivie.'

Abbey hesitated by the doctor's side as she
watched the smooth way he handled the oxy-viva and
assessed the infant. His hands were gentle and confident and she heaved a sigh of relief as she turned
away. He'd do.

'Why hasn't my baby cried?' Vivie craned her neck
anxiously to try and see her baby around the doctor's
broad back.

Abbey could sympathise. She wished the baby
would scream the place down. 'He's got a good
strong heart beat and is lovely and pink now, Vivie.
I don't know why he won't take a few big breaths of
his own, though. Sometimes babies take a couple of
minutes to change over to the outside world. Doctor

is keeping him well oxygenated until your son decides to breathe for himself.'

Vivie winced as she felt another contraction start in her uterus. 'You said all the pains would go away when I had my baby,' she accused the midwife. Abbey smiled.

'One more contraction is needed to push out your placenta and here it comes now. By the time we finish checking you, your baby should have woken up.'

The tension increased in the room as Abbey tidied Vivie in preparation to hold her baby. Finally a few faint cries were heard from the corner. Another minute passed and then Dr Roberts brought Vivie's baby across and placed him in her arms.

The joy in Vivie's face brought a lump to Abbey's throat—and a lot of painful memories. She glanced away and caught the doctor watching her.

Dr Roberts smiled and every woman in the room felt the radiant heat from it. Abbey was no exception so she blinked and turned away. Some lucky girl must sunbake under that smile, she thought to herself with an unusual touch of despondency.

'Your son is fine,' the doctor said. 'Probably just stunned from the birth. But his heart sounds normal and he's breathing well for himself now. I've had a good look at him and he's all present and accounted for. These two ladies will keep an eye on him over the next few hours but I shouldn't think you'll have any problems with the lad.'

His calm voice reassured Vivie and Abbey had to

admit the deep gravelly sound of it would have made his fortune on radio. Usually she could enjoy the presence of a handsome man without any of these asinine flutters that she'd thought she'd grown out of.

Vivie cuddled her new son next to her skin and Abbey settled the blankets around them both before she stepped back. The little boy gazed owlishly up at his mother and Abbey felt the tension ease from her shoulders because he was none the worse from his slow start.

Her attention was drawn back to the new doctor and her strange impression that his presence seemed to infiltrate the whole room. Suddenly Abbey needed to escape. 'Check baby's respirations every couple of minutes, would you, please, Michelle?' Abbey whispered. 'I'll nip out for a moment and write my version of the delivery up so Doctor can have the notes to write his.'

Michelle nodded and started to tidy the room. Abbey slipped out the door.

'Thank you, Doctor,' Vivie murmured, not taking her eyes from her son.

Rohan Roberts nodded and glanced around the room. The nurse was here but he couldn't see the midwife. He'd wanted to congratulate her on the calm manner of their resuscitation. He'd seen rooms more fraught with half a dozen medicos coping with the same situation. Yet what had needed to be done had been done without fuss, with only the two of them before he'd arrived. That was what he liked about country hospitals. The staff relied on their own resources without panicking.

He'd enjoy the next two weeks working here. You could usually tell by the vibes in a place how well it was run, and Gladstone Hospital Maternity Ward felt like a beauty. The midwife hadn't been bad either. Down, boy, he admonished himself with a wry grin.

Rohan crossed over to the sink in the corner of the room to wash his hands, then picked up his hat. He'd better get back to the surgery or the waiting room would be overflowing.

The nurse handed him a towel. 'Welcome to Gladstone. Thank you for coming, Doctor,' she said.

Rohan smiled and she smiled back. 'I think you had it in hand without me,' he said. Rohan played back the background conversation and surprisingly he could remember everything the absent midwife had said. 'It's Michelle, isn't it?'

Michelle blushed with pleasure and nodded. He held out his other hand and shook Michelle's. 'Rohan,' he said. 'Nice to meet you.' Then he waved his hat at Vivie and was gone.

The two women looked at each other and Michelle pretended to swoon onto the end of Vivie's bed. They both started to giggle.

At the sister's station, Abbey finished her notes as Rohan arrived. The hairs on the back of her neck tickled as he approached and a flutter of excitement under her rib cage made her frown. Reacting like this was ridiculous.

She looked at a point over his left shoulder and handed him the patient's chart as she edged past. She wasn't sure why it was so important not to come into contact with his body but she obeyed the instinct. 'Here you go, Doctor. I'll pop back down to the birthing suite. Thank you for coming.'

Rohan watched her walk away, couldn't not watch her, and he narrowed his eyes as he tried to work out why. She wasn't classically beautiful, more alluringly pretty with soft golden-brown eyes, tall but not slim like his usual taste in women, and there was something vulnerable and innocently sensual about the line of her neck under that ponytail of red hair—that touched him. And touched him in a spot that had been fiercely guarded for years. 'Sister?'

Abbey stopped and hesitated before she turned around. Reluctantly she faced him and the bland enquiry on her face belied the nervousness she was feeling. 'Yes?'

'Well done in there. I was most impressed with your calmness.' He smiled that sunbeam of a smile and there was no doubt that Abbey could feel the burn factor.

Abbey smiled wryly. 'I'm renowned for my calmness, Doctor. Thank you for coming.' Then she turned away and thought bitterly to herself that she wasn't feeling calm at all. She couldn't remember being flustered this much by a man for years. And she didn't want to be flustered now. There was something about the new Dr Roberts that jangled her nerves. She'd nearly made it to the safety of the birth suite when he called her again.

'One more thing...'

Abbey paused and twisted her suddenly stiff neck to look at him as she rested her hand on the door-handle. An intense expression drew his dark brows together as he came towards her, and Abbey quelled the flutter of panic. One strong hand held his hat against a powerful thigh and Abbey's gaze crossed his flat stomach and, fancifully, she imagined a low-slung holster on the other. Her eyes skittered upward for distraction and she catalogued that his hair was almost black—like his eyes. Calmness. Ha!

She took a deep breath, then removed her hand from the door as she turned to face him. This was her ward and her town. The thought steadied her and her fingers linked with seeming serenity in front of her stomach. 'Yes, Doctor?'

She was disconcerted when he stopped right in front of her and held out his hand. 'You haven't introduced yourself.'

Someone must have superglued her fingers together because when they finally untangled from their serene pose they came apart with a little jerk. She wondered if he'd noticed her reluctance to touch him but there was nothing Abbey could do but put her hand in his.

It wasn't too bad, holding his hand—disturbingly pleasant, in fact. His grip was firm with the right amount of pressure, strong but not trying to prove a point. You could tell a lot about a man from his handshake—Clayton's had been more in the dead-fish line. As the thought of her ex-fiancé drifted through Abbey's mind she blinked and stepped back to break the contact—and felt the door behind her back. Trapped.

'I'm Rohan and you are…?' His deep voice was even more beautiful when he lowered it.

'Abbey Wilson.' Brief, but at least she hadn't squeaked. Abbey straightened her spine and met his eyes. She'd had enough of what had to be some surface chemical reaction she was feeling from this man. 'Nursing Unit Manager.'

'Would that be Mrs Wilson or Miss?'

'Sister. And I really do have to get back to my patient.'

He ignored the last part of her comment and concentrated on the 'Sister'. His black eyes twinkled. 'So you're a nun?'

'As good as…' Abbey's voice was dry and she was in full control finally. 'Now, I do have to go.' She put her hand back on the door handle. 'Goodbye, Doctor.' She didn't look back as she turned away to enter the birth suite.

She heard him say, 'I'll just write up the notes, then,' as she closed the door gently.

Michelle and Vivie were still giggling when Abbey entered the room. She raised one eyebrow and they stopped like guilty schoolgirls. Abbey had to smile.

'You guys weren't tittering in here, were you?' Abbey said.

Michelle shrugged. 'With the exception of this lad's refusal to breathe…' she brushed a finger down Vivie's son's cheek '…getting smiled at by Dr Roberts is the most excitement Vivie and I have had for a long time. Eh, Vivie?'

Vivie sighed and nodded. 'I know you're happy being single, Abbey, but I'd love to have a man like that waiting at home for me. I think I'm going to call my son Rohan.'

Abbey bit her lip to stop her grin. Vivie had promised more than one man she'd name her son after him.

That evening, Abbey relaxed in her favourite chair in front of the fire in her study and stared through the glass at the amber coals. It was October and she probably didn't need a fire but she enjoyed the atmosphere it created.

Her German shepherd, Clive, rested his head on her feet. She'd found Clive as a puppy in a box, left outside her door, and of course she'd kept him. Despite his fetish for chewing shoes, he'd more than rewarded her with fierce loyalty. Abbey's study and kitchen were the only rooms Clive was allowed in and you could tell he loved the evenings with Abbey before he had to go outside for the night.

Abbey wasn't even aware of the pressure of Clive's head on her feet. She couldn't help remembering her encounter with the new doctor and she hoped the warmth she could feel in her cheeks was from the fire.

It was her reaction that grated and she really didn't want to travel that path again.

It had been almost ten years since she'd been foolishly attracted to another man and the pain that had followed had taught Abbey a cruel lesson.

In the year after their mother's death she'd been vulnerable and weighed down with the responsibility of two younger sisters and a rambling old house that had constantly needed repairs.

Abbey hadn't wanted to become involved with Clayton Harrows either. Debonair and supremely confident, Clayton had lulled her into thinking him so trustworthy, and she'd become unwillingly besotted by his attention to her.

He'd convinced Abbey to invest her mother's money with him so that there would be no problem funding her sisters through university.

When Clayton had asked Abbey to marry him she'd thought all her dreams had come true. It had been a whirlwind courtship and although the one time they'd made love had been an unpleasant disappointment, Abbey had refused to listen to her instincts. Awkwardly embarrassed with her impatient lover, Abbey had promised that aspect of their relationship would improve once they were married, and had managed to stave him off with that assurance.

She'd been such a fool and still been in love with the idea of love until the week before the wedding! Clayton had stayed late, after the girls were in bed, and had drunk his way through all her mother's port as he'd sat at the kitchen table. Then he'd revealed he'd lost her sisters' money, through some disastrous get-rich-quick scheme.

When he'd declared that a mortgage on Abbey's house would reverse all their fortunes, Abbey had begun to comprehend the enormity of her mistake. The more alcohol Clayton had imbibed, the more obnoxious he'd become, as if now that it had been too late for Abbey to back out he hadn't had to hide his true self.

Abbey couldn't disguise her revulsion at his increasingly coarse behaviour and her obvious disgust inflamed his temper. Perhaps he'd thought because Abbey had slept with him once before it wouldn't matter, but the smell of his drunken breath in her face as he viciously tried to force himself on her against her will stayed with Abbey for many years.

After a desperate struggle, Abbey threw him out of her house with the aid of a much younger but ferociously protective Clive, and Clayton retaliated by labelling her a frigid and a useless lover, words she carried with her still.

The next day, when Clayton had discovered she'd cancelled the wedding, he'd become so angry he'd threatened Abbey with violence until finally she'd again set her dog on him. When he'd threatened to return she'd laid charges against him and had then found out that he'd already been on a good behaviour bond for another incident and this time would go to gaol.

A week later, when Abbey discovered she was pregnant with Clayton's baby, a part of her wanted to curl up and die. She didn't have the time, so she told no one. With both sisters still in high school, she needed to provide for her family and in some way make up for her lack of judgement which had cost her sisters their inheritance.

When she lost the baby at nine weeks, the weight of guilt from denying the baby's existence almost suffocated her. The only person she'd told of the pregnancy had been her doctor, Scott Rainford, and after the miscarriage she locked those feelings away from the world.

She recovered her sense of purpose but the woman who emerged from that experience was changed for ever. As if forged in steel, Abbey's resolve to depend only on herself had never wavered.

Somehow, over the years, others came to appreciate that Abbey was the person to turn to in times of stress so that the wooden house in Chisholm Road was rarely without a temporary boarder.

Abbey could untangle the most complicated web of lies and reunite the most stubborn of lovers. Parents of teenagers sought Abbey's advice and the maternity ward she was in charge of ran smoothly, from housekeeping to nursing personnel. Even the doctors realised that Abbey's gently spoken word was law.

Abbey pulled the black elastic band from her hair and shook her head as if to banish the dark thoughts. She massaged her scalp with unsteady fingers. Equilibrium was all she wanted and she didn't need any blow-through tumbleweed of a locum upsetting her routine or her emotions.

Emotions were for the young and she was thirty-one, for pity's sake.

Which reminded her… Vivie was coming to stay in one of the spare rooms with her baby, and Aunt Sophie needed to be told.

In the huge front room, Aunt Sophie sat in front of her cable TV surrounded by TAB form guides as she watched the trots. Abbey smiled fondly at the spikes of silver hair that poked through the centre of her aunt's sunvisor headband.

'Aunt Sophie?'

Sophie turned her head towards Abbey but her eyes never left the screen. 'Hang on, I've fifty cents on this one. It's for you. It's called Maiden's Blush.'

Abbey shook her head and watched as Maiden's Blush trotted in equal last.

'Darn.' Sophie squinted up at Abbey and cackled. 'Should have taken My Dark Lord, like I was going to.' She lifted a pile of form guides off the over-stuffed chair beside her and patted the seat. 'Take a pew. You look tired.'

Abbey leaned across and kissed her aunt and sat down. She ignored Sophie's accusatory 'tired' comment. 'I need to talk to you about a new lodger I have coming in a couple of days.'

Sophie lifted one sparse eyebrow and nodded. 'Another lame duck, I suppose?'

'Vivie isn't a lame duck, she's a young friend of mine.' Abbey pretended to frown at her aunt but Sophie just cackled again.

'We're all lame ducks, sweetie, and your heart is too big. But who am I to cast the first stone? I'm one of them. Tell me about your friend, Vivie.'

Abbey shook her head, genuinely upset that her aunt felt she was a burden. 'Don't say that. You're the matriarch of the family and I can't imagine the house without you.'

'The shoe fits you better, Abbey, but get on with it. I've another race in five minutes and this one's a sure thing. Punter's Dream.' She grinned, hitched up her metal sleeve-holders to bunch her sleeves back from her wrists, then settled back in her chair to wait for Abbey's explanation.

Abbey gathered her thoughts. 'Vivie's eighteen and the oldest of five children. Her baby was born this morning and she's been living in a caravan since her widowed father found out she was pregnant. I don't think she should go back to the caravan park now that baby…Rohan is here.' Abbey hesitated over the name because it wasn't tiny blue baby eyes she thought of when she said it, but coal-black man's eyes. She forced her thoughts back to her aunt. 'So I offered to put her up here until she finds something better.'

Sophie snorted. 'So, hasn't she heard of birth control, and where's the baby's father?'

Abbey bit her lip. 'Vivie doesn't know who the baby's father is.' Before her aunt could say anything,

Abbey went on calmly, 'Vivie was drugged at a party she attended and doesn't remember the attack. She's the second local girl that I know of that this has happened to. Thankfully the other girl didn't fall pregnant but the situation was still horrendous for her.'

Sophie frowned and didn't even glance at the television as the next race started. 'In my day they'd whip scum like that. Has she been to the police?'

'Vivie was too embarrassed at the time but I hope to convince both girls to talk to each other and maybe do so in the future.' Abbey's empathy lay with the girls because she'd found it hard to go to the police after Clayton's attack. She sighed without realising it. Tonight had turned out to be a night for dark memories.

'Well, as an oldest child, no doubt she'll be good at handling babies. I'll make your friend and her babe welcome, though I'm not much good with tiny ones. Which room are you putting them in?'

'I thought I'd offer Mum's old room. I don't want my sisters to think I've moved them out of their rooms when they come home.'

Sophie nodded and then noticed her horse race had started. She frowned and turned up the volume control. 'Come on, Punters Dream!'

Abbey compressed her lips to control her amusement as her aunt jiggled about on the seat urging her horse on to victory. As Punter's Dream passed the post first, Sophie pumped her fist in the air and turned a gap-toothed grin at Abbey. 'That's six dollars I've won for my fifty cents.'

Abbey shook her head. 'Do you ever finish out of pocket?'

Sophie shrugged. 'Sometimes, that's the nature of gambling.' She grinned wickedly. 'But I can back three race meetings with eight races each for twelve dollars. And I've a fair nest egg to show for it.' Her aunt narrowed her eyes and all amusement left her face. 'You won't struggle for money again, Abbey. I'll never forget you taking me in when you had too much on your plate already.'

Abbey stood up and leaned over to kiss her aunt goodnight. 'You're a national treasure, and I can't imagine the house without you. Goodnight.'

CHAPTER TWO

ROHAN ROBERTS parked his new Range Rover outside Maternity and switched off the radio. The strains
of the country ballad lingered in his mind and brought
back distant memories of his childhood in Tamworth.
The hotel bar his mother had worked in had played
that song over and over again and it seemed strange
to hear it without the smell of beer or raucous voices
in the background.

He'd been fourteen when she'd died. His mother
had always seemed to collect losers and no-hopers
who'd needed her help. This final time the woman in
need had gone to sleep with a lit cigarette and had
burned his mother's house down. Ironically, the
woman who'd caused it all had managed to escape.
His mother had refused to leave the burning building
until she'd found and saved Rohan, though she'd been
overcome with smoke soon after and had perished
herself. He'd never stopped feeling guilty that he
hadn't made her go first.

Even now he could taste the anger he'd felt as a
lost teenager. Anger that his mother had allowed
someone who hadn't cared whether they lived or died
to take her away from him. Anger at himself for not
saving her. With maturity he could see it all had been

bad luck or maybe a tragic fate, but his tolerance for those who needed propping by others remained limited.

He slammed the door of his car and absently ran his hand down the shiny black duco of the car next to his. The old Willys was a beauty, considering her age, and shrieked character. Parked beside the Range Rover, the old car made his own car look soulless. Rohan shrugged. That was a car for people who'd planted roots so deep they'd never move on.

The first person he saw when he opened the door was Abbey Wilson. It was funny how he knew who it was.

She was bending over a portable baby cot, making it up with clean sheets. Her back was towards him and it was only natural that his eyes strayed to the delightful picture she presented. Long, shapely legs and a delectably rounded bottom that promised no sharp edges.

One part of him sighed in pleasure that she was here and another warned of an unhealthy fixation with a woman who would not be interested in his type of dalliance.

'Good morning, Sister Abbey.' He watched her straighten with a jerk and interestingly she lifted her hand to her hair before she snatched it away again. Her lovely mouth firmed and she glared at him.

Rohan suppressed his amusement and glanced at his watch as if he had to be somewhere urgently, which he didn't, before he moved towards the desk.

'It's not Sister Abbey, it's Sister Wilson or Abbey,' she said. She regained her composure quickly. He could tell that by her voice and her businesslike move to the desk to gather the charts for the ward round.

He'd achieved what he'd wanted. 'My apologies, Abbey.' Her name felt good when he said it and she was wearing some citrus perfume that could make him look at oranges in a whole new, sensual light. He'd never been so aware of the little things about a woman before. He pondered that. Usually his interest remained with the obvious, but the allure of Abbey Wilson was more subtle and each tantalising glimpse of her character drew him deeper into the unfamiliar—a bit like heading into the bush without a compass—fascinating but dangerous.

He'd thought of her too many times over the last twenty-four hours and here he was cataloging more things to remember. Better to do what he was supposed to be doing and then get out of here.

He slapped his hat down on the desk and derided himself. Move. Rohan inclined his head towards the patient rooms. 'Let's go do the ward round, then. What are we waiting for?'

They walked up the hallway together and Abbey seethed. She hadn't been the one to stare blankly at a chart in a daydream! And that 'Sister Abbey' stuff had been a ruse to trick her into allowing him to call her by her first name. The guy needed watching.

Vivie looked up as they entered her room, and she

blushed when she saw it was the doctor. It made her look younger than the eighteen Abbey knew she was.

'Good morning, Vivie.' Rohan's voice was friendly and he leaned over the cot and ran his hand gently over Vivie's baby's scalp as if he loved the feel. Abbey couldn't help noticing his tenderness and it gave her a funny pain low down in her stomach. How strange that no such feelings had surfaced when Scott had patted an infant. She watched his face as he saw the name card on the cot. 'You called him Rohan?' He smiled at Vivie and the girl's blush deepened. 'I'm flattered.'

Abbey rolled her eyes as if to say vanity was a sin and he winked cheekily and turned back to the patient.

'So you're feeling well, Vivie?' Vivie nodded, tongue-tied, and Abbey stepped into the silence.

'Vivie's postnatally well and she's mastering the art of breastfeeding more each feed. She wants to stay another day or two before she goes home.'

'Sounds fine to me,' said Rohan. 'I'll come back and see you tomorrow, then. About this time?' Vivie nodded and Abbey and Rohan moved on to the next room.

After seeing the four other patients who had been under the care of Scott Rainford, Rohan accompanied Abbey back to the desk. As they walked, she was aware of his height as he strode beside her, aware of the strength in his hands, which was tempered by his gentle handling of babies, and the tangy scent of some expensive aftershave that she had the horrible feeling she would always associate with him. She didn't need to notice these things.

He jiggled his keys in his pocket, and seemed to hesitate, then said, 'Is that your old Willys out there?'

Abbey blinked. 'Er...?' Her mind searched for enlightenment. Abbey blinked again. She had no idea what he was talking about.

He was serious about the question. 'The black car.'

The light clicked on and she chuckled. 'I thought you said wellies, as in gumboots.' She looked down at her feet and back at him. 'You mean Doris?'

It was his turn to look confused.

'The Willys. It's my aunt's car but she doesn't have a licence any more. We call her Doris and, yes, I drive her now.'

He nodded. 'The car suits you,' he said cryptically, picked up his hat, lifted his hand in a salute and was gone.

Abbey walked slowly behind the desk and sat down. 'OK,' she said out loud, and sighed. He was just too sinfully good-looking and he did have some sense of humour, but that didn't mean she was going to turn to jelly every time he came to the ward.

The phone rang and she snatched it up with relief. After a brief discussion, she put the phone down again and rose to her feet. One of her antenatal class couples were coming in with early labour signs and hopefully they would keep her nicely busy for the rest of the day.

*   *   *

In his office, Rohan's thoughts weren't on the room full of patients he had yet to see. He was staring at the computer screen, telling the shadowy reflection of his face that he wasn't interested in pursuing a self-confessed nun in a place he was just passing through.

His rules were simple. Stick to the fun-loving girls who knew the score, because he was never going to marry or stay in one place. He had no intention of burdening someone with the guilt he still carried around from his mother.

Scott would be back in less than two weeks and he'd be better occupied caring for his friend's patients than mooning over the sweetest face. He frowned. When had he decided that Abbey's face was the sweetest?

Rohan pushed himself out of the chair and walked over to call in his next patient.

At three o'clock, Abbey handed the ward keys over to the evening staff and pushed open the door to a glorious afternoon. She felt the tiredness seep away from her shoulders and drew a deep breath of the spring air. Everything seemed brighter this afternoon for some reason.

Abbey climbed into Aunt Sophie's Doris and the old car moved with stately precision into the traffic. She hummed a tune from the CD the birthing couple had brought in for their labour.

They had chosen this particular song to be playing at the time of their baby's birth. Abbey had felt a little like an actor fluffing her lines when she'd had to keep repeating the song to catch the actual moment of birth, but it had been worth it.

As she drove slowly down the main street, she couldn't help her gaze drifting towards the building that housed Scott's surgery—and Rohan. She wondered what he was doing. Up ahead, the screech of rubber drew her eyes quickly back to the road and she slammed on the brakes.

Doris creaked and groaned but obediently ground to a halt only a few centimetres from possible disaster. The car on the opposite side of the road had suffered an even more dramatically sudden stop and sat, with tyres smoking, at a crazy angle to the white line in the centre of the busy street. The driver leaned out of his window and gestured at the woman who'd crossed dangerously in front of him, almost causing a pile-up. The young, heavily pregnant woman had dark smudges of mascara down her cheeks and as she crossed to Abbey's side of the street, oblivious to the chaos, she blew her nose. She stared over Doris's long bonnet into Abbey's shocked eyes and realised that all the traffic had stopped because of her.

'I'm sorry,' she mouthed, and put her hand on Doris's bonnet to push herself towards the footpath.

Abbey flipped out the blinker arm and pulled over into the next parking space. Her hands were shaking and she swallowed a lump of fear that had lodged in her throat. If the screech of the other driver's brakes hadn't drawn her attention… If Doris hadn't been able to stop… If the girl had been walking faster…

There were a lot of ifs, but it was still too close to the fact that Abbey hadn't been paying enough attention to the road and could have hit the woman. She closed her eyes for a moment and then glanced in the rear-view mirror to spot the young woman as she stumbled down the footpath.

Hurriedly Abbey opened the door and clambered down onto the street without checking the traffic. There was another shriek of brakes as a truck full of cattle rumbled past too close for comfort. It really wouldn't help if she caused her own accident, Abbey chastised herself as she hurried after the girl.

'Excuse me?' Abbey put her hand on the girl's shoulder and the young woman shuddered in fright and stopped. When she turned and saw it was Abbey she relaxed a little.

'I said I was sorry,' the girl mumbled, and Abbey quickly shook her head.

'No, no. It was my fault. I wasn't watching the road as carefully as I should and nearly hit you.' Abbey was assessing the girl for any injuries and thankfully she couldn't see any. Judging by the streaks of make-up on her face, she'd been crying for a while. She was wearing one of those inexpensive silver necklaces with her name in cursive. Kayla. At least Abbey knew her name now.

Kayla sniffed. 'The other car came closer but I really don't care.'

She didn't care! Warning bells rang and Abbey searched for an excuse to detain Kayla until she could find some help. 'Do you live near here? Can I take you to your home?'

The young woman's face contorted and she started to sob. 'I don't have a home. He threatened me and I left.' Kayla turned beseeching eyes to Abbey and Abbey's soft heart was torn by the fear in the young woman's face. Abbey blinked away the tears that misted her own eyes. Without thought she stepped closer and gathered Kayla into her arms just as Rohan came up behind Kayla.

'Hell, that was close, Abbey. What were you thinking?' He spoke over Kayla's head and glared at her, as if Abbey didn't feel bad enough.

'I didn't hit her, Doctor.' Abbey couldn't find anything else to say and she couldn't understand why Rohan only looked angrier.

'Hit who? That cattle truck nearly smeared you all over the road.' He looked from Abbey to the girl who had just realised there was a third party present and stepped back out of Abbey's arms.

Rohan wasn't satisfied. 'What did you think I was talking about?'

Abbey sighed and brushed the hair off her forehead. She had the beginnings of a headache from all the confusion and drama.

She sighed and gestured to the girl beside her. 'Kayla here...' She looked at the girl. 'It is Kayla, isn't it?'

Kayla nodded and started to back suspiciously away. 'How did you know?'

Abbey smiled reassuringly and pointed to the girl's necklace. 'I guessed.' She indicated Rohan. 'This is Dr Roberts.' She spoke to Rohan. 'I nearly ran over Kayla a moment ago and we were just going to have a coffee to settle our nerves.'

Kayla didn't dispute the coffee idea and Abbey almost sagged with relief that the girl wasn't going to run away. She looked at Rohan. 'So you can go back to your surgery and we'll go on our way.'

Rohan turned from Abbey to the girl and it was obvious he'd taken in her well-progressed pregnancy and agitated state.

'It might be better,' he said, 'if we all go back to my surgery and sit down there. Abbey can make coffee and I can have a listen to Kayla's baby's heartbeat and maybe take her blood pressure.'

He smiled his killer smile at Kayla and the girl almost smiled back. 'If I'm not mistaken, your feet are a little swollen as well, aren't they, Kayla?'

Kayla shrugged, but the fluid in her ankles was indisputable. 'I don't have anywhere else to go.'

So Abbey found herself making coffee in the tiny kitchen off the hallway from Rohan's consulting room. Through the open door she could see Kayla being fussed over by a handsome man, which, judging by her bemused expression, was something she wasn't used to.

When Abbey came in with the coffee, they'd ascertained that Kayla hadn't actually seen a doctor through her pregnancy, and didn't really know when her baby was due. Rohan ordered blood tests and an ultrasound and Abbey promised she'd accompany the girl later that afternoon, because Kayla began to look overwhelmed again.

'Where do you live, Kayla?' Rohan's question cemented an idea that had been forming in Abbey's mind as she'd hovered at one side of the room.

Abbey answered. 'Kayla's had to move out of her house and might decide to stay with me for a while.' She looked across at the girl who looked from Rohan to Abbey with relief. 'If you'd like to, Kayla?'

Kayla nodded slowly and some of the worry seeped from her face. 'If I could? Just until I sort myself out.'

Rohan's eyes widened and then narrowed. He pierced Abbey with a hard stare and jerked his head towards the hallway. 'You have your coffee, Kayla. I want to speak to Sister Wilson for a moment.' His voice gentled and he said, 'We'll sort it out, don't worry.'

What was his problem? Abbey considered refusal but, judging by the expression on his face when he looked at her, he might frogmarch her out there if she didn't go of her own free will.

She smiled reassuringly at Kayla. 'Enjoy your coffee. I'll be back for mine in a minute.' She shot a glare at Rohan and then preceded him from the room and across the hall to the kitchen.

It was a bad choice because the room was so small

and, with Rohan in there, Abbey felt as if she could hardly breathe.

'What the hell do you think you're doing?' Rohan's voice was almost a whisper but Abbey heard every word.

She tilted her chin at him. 'That's twice you've sworn at me. I won't tolerate it.'

Rohan blinked and ran back over what he'd said. '"Hell"? That's not swearing.'

Abbey stood her ground. 'As far as I'm concerned it is, so please refrain in my presence.'

Rohan shrugged. Was this woman for real? 'Sorry. I forgot. Convent Abbey.' He turned sideways a little to rest one powerful hip on the edge of the kitchen bench and effectively block the exit. 'But you won't distract me from what I have to say.'

He crossed his arms and the fabric of his shirt stretched across his chest. Abbey could see the delineation of his muscles and annoyingly that fluttery feeling was back in her stomach.

Rohan's expression was stern. 'Let me see if I have this right. You have never met this girl before today. She has mysteriously lost her place of residence and if I guess correctly she has probably left some less-than-savoury partner who may or may not come looking for her.

'Then, because you nearly run her down, you feel obliged to provide a roof over her head for an indefinite time and run her from pathology to ultrasound when ever she needs you to.'

He stopped and glanced cynically across at Abbey. 'Is that right?'

Abbey was trying to ignore how close he was in the small room, but his words seeped through the mist in her brain. One word jarred. 'Not "obliged". There is no obligation—just the normal empathy of one woman for another.' Abbey's voice firmed. 'I'd be happy to help her.'

She sidled back as far as the kitchenette allowed her and then drew herself up to her full five feet seven and met his eyes. 'And it's really none of your business.'

Rohan stifled some obvious swear word under his breath well enough for Abbey not to guess what it was. 'Come on, Abbey. She could be anyone. She could be a drug user or a kleptomaniac or even worse. And if there is some domestic issues or even domestic violence, it could all find its way into your house. Do you want that?'

Abbey couldn't understand why Rohan was labouring the point. 'I don't believe I have to worry about any of those things with Kayla. But if they are issues with her...' She paused and her voice was implacable. 'Then she needs my help more than I imagined and I will be there for her if she needs me.'

Rohan couldn't believe it. It was his mother all over again. What was it with women? He just hoped to hell—he felt like shouting the word—that Abbey didn't end up the way his mother had because he wouldn't be here to save her either.

He needed to get out of this situation right here and now. If Scott could be called back now, Rohan would be out of that door so fast his feet wouldn't touch the ground.

But all he said was, 'It's your funeral.' Rohan winced as he walked away. If he could have changed anything he'd said today it would have been that last word.

Later, after Kayla had had all her tests and Abbey had collected a few necessities for her from the supermarket, they went home to meet Abbey's aunt.

'And this is my Aunt Sophie. She owns Doris, the car we drove home in.' Abbey introduced Kayla as a guest and Sophie nodded without showing any surprise.

'Hello, Kayla. I haven't driven that car for many a year—it belongs to Abbey.' She looked up at Abbey with a twinkle in her eye and when Abbey refused to be drawn into an old fight she went on, 'And where are you going to put this one?'

Abbey shook her head at her aunt's teasing and smiled at her guest. 'Don't worry about Aunt Sophie. She has a good heart even if the outside is a bit gruff.'

She turned back to her aunt. 'I thought the room next door to Vivie's room.'

Sophie chuckled, waved them away and reached for her form guide. 'Sounds perfect. We could have a nursery for the babies and call them B1 and B2.'

The next morning Abbey couldn't help glancing at the clock. Rohan—Dr Roberts, she corrected herself—was due in around eight and she was determined to be efficiently collected, no matter what provocation he offered. She still smarted over his interference over her choice to offer Kayla accommodation and she decided she would refuse to be drawn into any more non-work-related conversations.

The outside door opened and Abbey fiddled with the papers in front of her as if she hadn't heard his footsteps approach.

'Good morning, Sister Wilson.' Rohan looked at the charts in Abbey's hands and then at his watch. His hat appeared on top of the desk and his voice was cooler and more detached than she'd heard it before.

As Abbey rose to hand him the charts she couldn't help the contrary whisper of disappointment at the distance in his manner. 'Good morning, Doctor,' she said. 'We have two women going home this morning and I need checks on their babies prior to discharge.'

Rohan nodded, still not looking at her, and started down the corridor. 'I'll do the ward round first and we can finish in the nursery, then.'

Abbey frowned as she followed his tall figure. His manner was an about-face from the open friendliness of yesterday and she assured herself she preferred it that way. Then to her horror she heard herself say, 'So you can be as moody as every other man.'

Rohan stopped abruptly and Abbey had to swerve not to run into him. As she came level he turned his head. She didn't care for the sardonic lift of his eyebrows as this time he looked at her fully—head to toe in a sweeping assessment that left nothing out—and she blushed.

'So you blush as well?' The tone of his voice held more than a tinge of mockery, whether directed at her or at himself she couldn't tell.

But the demon inside Abbey, one she hadn't realised she had, relished the danger this conversation contained. Her eyebrows rose. 'As well as what, Doctor?'

He spread his arms. 'Run a ward, handle obstetric crises, save people from the streets and put doctors in their place when their manners are lacking in politeness.' His voice hardened. 'You're a bloody marvel.'

Abbey felt as if she'd been slapped. The arrogant pig. He could see the patients himself. Her voice was calm but cool. 'Well, enjoy the round. This "marvel" will be at the desk if you want me, Doctor.' She turned on her heel and left him.

Rohan gazed at the ceiling. He'd intended to create distance between them but that had been unforgivable. What was it about this woman that tipped him off balance? He'd never set out to upset anyone before but, then, no one had endangered his peace of mind like Abbey did—and with such ease.

His life suited him. A couple of weeks here, a few months there, no commitments and more than enough money to provide the possessions in life that he'd dreamed of as a child. And no emotional entanglements! He didn't need a conscience wrapped up in a sister's uniform to illustrate how shallow his life was.

Unfortunately, he couldn't forget her stricken look and he felt like a louse. No doubt he would feel worse later if he didn't do something about it.

When he went back to the desk she ignored him as she filled out the bed statement list. The air was two degrees cooler down this end of the corridor.

He stared at her for a moment but she refused to acknowledge him. He gave up waiting for her and practised his charm. 'Abbey. I'm sorry.'

She ignored him.

Crashed and burned. He couldn't remember the last time he'd apologised to anyone but he'd bet it had been successful. Maybe he was out of practice.

He put his hand on her shoulder and it was warm and firm under his palm. He resisted the urge to run his fingertips over that line of her neck that intrigued him. He could imagine that would go over like a lead balloon.

'I shouldn't have sworn, and I won't in the future. Come and do the round with me and then I'll get out of your hair.'

Abbey looked up at him and tried to ignore the heat of his hand seeping into her. At least he'd shown his true colours early in the piece and she knew this apology was all part of the fake-charming act. She stood up abruptly and the move made his hand fall away.

'Apology accepted.' She didn't smile as she walked past him and gathered up the charts again. He followed and she could feel his eyes burning into her neck all the way up the corridor.

Abbey said little for most of the round until they came to Vivie, who was sitting out of bed with her baby in her arms.

'So, Vivie,' Rohan said, 'how are the two of you doing?'

Vivie glanced at Abbey and then licked her lips to summon up the nerve to speak. 'Fine, thank you, Doctor.' She looked at her son in her arms and her voice strengthened. 'He's a good boy.'

She smiled at her baby and Rohan smiled with her. 'Of course he is. He's got a good mum,' he said.

Vivie flushed with pleasure and Abbey could almost forgive him anything when he was like this.

Rohan checked the baby's feed chart. 'So, when were you thinking of going home?'

'Tomorrow or the next day, if it's all right with you. Though we're not going home to the caravan park.' Vivie looked at Abbey. 'We're moving to Abbey's until we find somewhere better than the caravan to live.'

Abbey saw him close his eyes for a moment.

'Of course you are,' he said with an admirable lack of expression.

CHAPTER THREE

ROHAN raised his eyebrows at Abbey and she knew what he was thinking. When he asked Vivie, 'So how long have you known Abbey?' Abbey could have strangled him.

'Abbey was my antenatal class teacher.' She turned shining eyes to her idol. 'She's wonderful.'

'I'm sure she is,' he said dryly. 'I'll check baby tomorrow and then you can decide when you're ready to leave.'

Unaware of the undercurrents, Vivie nodded, at peace with her world.

Abbey accompanied Rohan back to the nursery where she handed him the neonatal stethoscope for the pre-discharge infant examinations. She watched him unwrap and examine one of the babies with the care and attention she was beginning to expect from him. His hands were gentle yet thorough and when he'd assured the mother that her baby was well and without any abnormalities, everyone believed him and smiled with him.

Even Abbey, until she realised she was falling under his spell again. To distract herself she handed him the infant's record book to fill out.

He washed his hands and then repeated the procedure on the second child. Abbey relaxed slightly and began to hope he wasn't going to say anything about Vivie's plans.

Well, why should he? she thought as she cleaned the stethoscope before hanging it back up on the infant resuscitation trolley. They both needed to work with each other for the next ten days before Scott came back, and she'd made it clear she didn't want his opinion on Kayla.

The second mother left the nursery reassured and that left Rohan and Abbey in the big room alone. The tension in the air went up a notch as the silence lengthened. Rohan leaned back against the window-sill, quite at ease. Then he said, 'I'm intrigued.'

'Really?' Abbey's heart rate jumped ten beats. Maybe she'd been premature in her wishful thinking but she wasn't playing his game if she could help it.

'I'm sure it's no business of mine, but just how many people do you have checked into your little convalescent refuge, slash, home away from home?'

Despite a spurt of irritation, Abbey refused to be drawn. 'I'm so pleased you agree it's none of your business,' she said, and walked out of the nursery before her unruly tongue could get her into more trouble.

Now all she needed was for him to go. But he didn't. He followed her back to the desk and leant against it.

Abbey turned her head stiffly and looked at him. 'Was there anything else you wanted, Doctor?'

He sighed, clearly exasperated. 'I really don't know why I'm persisting with this. But I have had some experience of the disadvantages of being a good Samaritan, Abbey, and I wonder if you know what can happen.'

Abbey raised her eyebrows. 'Somehow, you and the words "good Samaritan" don't seem synonymous to me.'

To stay was obviously hopeless but Rohan thought of his mother, and even the tiniest chance of Abbey ending up like her meant he couldn't leave. Especially Abbey. Though why—especially Abbey—he hadn't figured out yet.

He tried one last time. 'So how do I stop you looking at me in that supercilious way, Sister Wilson?'

Abbey raised her eyebrows even higher and glanced at the clock. 'You could leave.'

Rohan winced. He stood up. He didn't need this. 'For a nun, you're not very forgiving.'

'For a doctor, you don't mind keeping your patients waiting.'

When he left, her shoulders slumped with the release of tension. What a fiasco! So much for being calm and collected. She'd behaved like a child. It was so unlike her but he set her nerves twitching and she couldn't help it.

Later that day, after work, it had been arranged for Abbey to take Kayla to collect her possessions. Trevor, Kayla's ex-boyfriend, was usually well ensconced at the local pub at that time, and hopefully the flat would be empty when they arrived.

When they pulled up in Doris, Kayla seemed reluctant to get out of the safety of the car and Abbey began to have second thoughts about the wisdom of their visit without suitable reinforcements.

'If you're worried that Trevor might become unpleasant then I'm happy to ask the police to meet us here, Kayla.' Abbey lifted her mobile phone from her bag and laid it on the dashboard to reinforce her words.

Kayla bit her lip and shook her head. 'No police.'

Abbey sighed. 'You're sure, even if he came home unexpectedly, he's not going to cause any trouble?'

'No,' Kayla said in a small voice.

'No, what?' Abbey sighed again. 'No, he won't cause any trouble or, no, you're not sure if he will?'

Kayla drew a deep breath and opened her door. 'If you don't want to come with me, it's OK, Abbey. I'll go on my own.'

'No, you won't.' Abbey slid her phone into her pocket and climbed out. 'But I'll be happier when we're out of here.'

'Me, too.' Kayla's response didn't do anything to alleviate Abbey's misgivings but she followed the girl across the street.

They climbed the stairs to the second floor without passing any neighbours, and when Kayla knocked on the door with its peeling paintwork there was no answer from within.

The two women looked at each other and then Kayla slid the key into the lock and pushed open the door. It squeaked ominously.

All doors creak in old buildings, Abbey reassured herself as she followed her new friend into the dark and odorous room. Grease-stained take-away food wrap lay on the worn carpet. Kayla stepped over some newspapers and a collection of empty spirit bottles, then disappeared into the only bedroom, leaving Abbey alone in the room.

If she'd had any doubts about taking Kayla in, those doubts were emphatically removed. This was no place to bring up a baby.

Kayla reappeared with two plastic shopping bags of baby clothes and a pair of sneakers that had seen better days. 'It's usually not this untidy. Let's get out of here,' she said, but it was too late. A thin, wild-eyed young man burst into the room and both women jumped in fright.

His roughened feet were bare of shoes and his grubby hands stretched out between them and the doorway to the outside. 'Caught ya! What d'ya think ya doin'?' he growled at Kayla, and she pulled the bags up in front of her stomach protectively.

Abbey drew a steadying breath. She edged slowly towards Kayla without taking her eyes off the man in the middle of the room, not sure what she hoped to achieve but positive that two women together were better than one.

His bloodshot eyes swung towards Abbey. 'Who're

you?' Little balls of foam flecked the side of his mouth and Abbey suppressed a shiver at the thought of trying to be rational with this man.

Abbey spoke slowly and forced her voice to a level and reasonable tone. 'I'm Kayla's friend and we came to get a few of her things. We're leaving now.'

As she spoke she edged closer to Kayla and pulled her gently towards the door past him. They made an awkward shuffling progress around the walls of the room and Abbey watched Trevor's face as he slowly processed what she'd said. She could tell the exact moment the message sank in because his eyes narrowed and he suddenly took a lunging stride towards them.

Abbey pushed Kayla out the door and almost made it through herself before he grabbed her arm and yanked her back against his body.

Abbey gasped in shock and hot points of pain erupted in her wrist where he gripped her. Her instinct screamed to get out fast and without further thought she stamped down on his foot as hard as she could to loosen his hold. Then she wrenched herself free and bolted down the stairs after Kayla. Her heart thumped in her chest as the release of adrenaline coursed around her body and her breath hissed in short gasps. Abbey caught up with Kayla on the pavement and took her arm to help her hurry awkwardly across the road and climb into Doris. Breasts heaving, they looked at each other in relief at gaining the car's safety.

Abbey glanced up at the building as they drove off and she could see Trevor watching them from the window and caught the shake of his fist.

'I'm so sorry, Abbey.' Kayla started to cry and Abbey patted the girl's leg. She should have listened to her second thoughts of calling the police but it was too late now.

'It's OK. It's over and we got what we came for.' She glanced across at Kayla and smiled unsteadily. 'And we're not going back.'

'When Trevor's sober, he's not too bad.' Kayla's voice was barely a whisper and Abbey rotated her neck to loosen the tension there.

Abbey pulled a face. 'Since you say he spends most days at the pub, I think you might live without the delightful side that attracted you to him.'

Kayla's half-laugh was pretty poor but Abbey admired her for the attempt. 'Thanks for coming with me, Abbey,' she said.

'I won't say it was a pleasure but I'm glad you didn't go alone. Let's get home and forget all about him. You deserve better than him, Kayla, and you need to remember that.'

Kayla drew a deep breath and stared out the front windscreen. 'My baby deserves better as well. I'm never going back.'

The next morning, Abbey was so busy in the labour ward she forgot to worry about when Rohan was due in. When he stuck his head in the door of birthing

unit, she'd just settled her client in the shower to help
relax her and had tidied the room.

'Have you time for a ward round, Sister Wilson?'
He'd decided that cool friendliness was the way to
go. In just over a week he'd be gone and worrying
about Abbey was annoying her and taking up too
many of his thoughts.

He saw her glance at the closed bathroom door and
then the clock. She opened the bathroom door a little
to poke her head through. 'I'm off to do a ward round,
Celia. If you or Eric want me, just press the buzzer.
Press it once and I'll come, press it twice and I'll
run—OK?'

He heard the assent from the shower and smiled at
her terminology. When she slipped out the door to
join him he couldn't help teasing her.

'I must ring the bell twice before I leave this place.
Just to see you run.'

'Ha! No chance.' Her eyes were more gold than
brown today and she had a delightful dimple at the
side of her mouth that he had a ridiculous urge to
trace. He tore his attention away from her face and
handed her the charts he held. Then he saw the ugly,
what could only be finger-mark bruises on her wrist.

The black rage that filled him came out of nowhere
like a satanic wraith. All the memories of the people
who'd hurt his mother while she'd tried to help them
welled up and consolidated into a fury directed at the
person who'd manhandled Abbey enough to cause her

skin to bruise. He wanted to know who—so he could grind them to a pulp!

Rohan's chest actually hurt with the effort to control his demand for an explanation when he knew he had no right to demand one. He sucked a lungful of air to calm himself down. This was crazy. He barely knew the woman.

Abbey felt him stiffen beside her and she glanced up to see what was wrong. His eyes had darkened to black slate and the expression in them actually frightened her. 'Rohan, what's wrong?' Then she saw him staring at the marks on her arm. Her other hand crossed to hide her wrist, and the forgotten charts slid from her fingers onto the floor. Glad of the distraction, she stooped to pick them up.

'What happened to your wrist, Abbey?' His voice was ominously quiet and rigid with control, and if she hadn't seen his eyes she might have answered him with the truth.

She didn't look up from the charts on the floor as she worried how best to deal with his reaction. He did have this thing about Kayla. The less he knew might be the more sensible thing. 'It's nothing.'

'Bull…' He paused and drew a deep breath. 'Droppings!'

'Droppings?' She flicked a look at him in incredulity then looked down again. 'Droppings?' She repeated it to herself and couldn't help a secret delighted smile at his restraint.

His smile was strained. 'I wouldn't like to sully your ears.'

She stood up and met the for once serious expression in his eyes. It was ridiculous to tell lies. 'Thank you for not swearing.' She kept her voice light. 'I had a minor tussle with Kayla's boyfriend when we went to pick up her stuff. But it all ended well.'

He took her hand and rubbed the pad of his thumb gently over the marks. 'You have deep bruising to your wrist. How does that constitute a minor tussle and ending up well?' His words were still clipped but Abbey was having trouble breathing from the sensations he was arousing in places other than her wrist. She tugged at her hand and he let go.

Suddenly she could breathe again and she walked up the corridor to gain a few seconds to clear her brain and put some distance between them.

'We got away!' Her over-the-shoulder throw-away line didn't have the desired result. In two strides he was in front of her and planted his feet so she couldn't go any further.

'Stop!' He looked up as if for inspiration, closed his eyes for a second and then opened them to impale her with an icy disbelief. 'You went with Kayla, by yourselves, no male escort, no police, to her flat, to confront her violent boyfriend?'

Abbey shook her head impatiently. 'We didn't go to confront him. We went to get her clothes. He was supposed to be drinking in the pub and not turn up.'

He shook his head. 'He should have been at the

pub? I see. What a masterful plan! I can't understand how it could have gone wrong.' He threw his head back and prayed to the Ceiling God again. Then he looked down at her. 'Are you mad? Why didn't you ask a man to go with you? For pity's sake, why didn't you ask me?'

Abbey stepped sideways away from his body. It was getting too darned warm, being that close to him. He was carrying on ridiculously and she had to get back to the birthing suite.

'Look. Rohan. Dr Roberts.' She used her calm and sensible voice as if he were a psychiatric patient. 'In retrospect it may have been a little unwise, but we survived, and it's really none of your business. And I won't be doing it again.'

The buzzer from the birthing suite glowed on and Abbey shrugged in barely concealed relief. 'Michelle's in the nursery if you want someone to do the round with you, but I have to go.' She handed him back the charts.

Rohan felt like slamming the charts against the wall in frustration. 'I can manage by myself. I'll see Michelle when I check Vivie's baby. But I haven't finished with you.'

Abbey made some small sound of disgust and left him.

Rohan watched her hurry back the way she'd come with a troubled frown. She had no idea what people were capable of, that was her problem. His problem was that he did know what people were capable of.

When he went in to see Vivie, she had a suitcase on the bed. Obviously she was ready to take her baby out of the hospital—to Abbey's house. How poetic.

'Hello, Vivie. Leaving today, I see.'

Vivie looked up when he entered her room and then she glanced at the door. Rohan correctly deduced her thoughts. 'Abbey's with a woman in labour so I have to do the round on my own today. How's my namesake?'

Vivie nodded and looked at her son. 'He's good. Now.' She smiled ruefully. 'He didn't sleep until early this morning but now my milk has come in Abbey said he'll be more settled.'

Rohan gestured to the vacant chair. 'Do you mind if I sit with you for a minute?'

Vivie stared for a moment and then shook her head. 'Of course not.'

It was underhand but he couldn't see how he was ever going to find out about Abbey's other life if he didn't ask someone. Not that he needed to know— but it might help him understand why she affected him the way she did if he had a little background knowledge. 'So you'll go home when Abbey finishes work this afternoon?'

Vivie nodded. 'She said the afternoon is a good time to go home, anyway.'

'I imagine it is. Not too much of a day to get through before you can safely go to bed.' He smiled. 'Have you been to Abbey's house?'

Vivie shook her head. 'Abbey only offered me a

room when I was in labour. But I know she lives with her elderly aunt and another girl has just moved in. Her house is at the top of the hill and used to be a boarding house. It's number seven.'

Rohan nodded as if he knew that. Satisfied, he filed the information away. 'Is there anything you're worried about, before you take your baby home?'

Vivie shook her head. 'I've had a bit to do with babies. My mother died and I've four younger brothers. And Abbey will be there.'

He stood up. 'I'm sure you'll manage beautifully. I'll be around for the next week or so. I can always pop in and see young Rohan after work one day if you have any concerns.'

Vivie looked startled, as well she might. 'Thank you, Doctor.'

Rohan smiled. 'Any friend of Abbey's is a friend of mine. When you're ready, if you'd like to wheel his cot down to the nursery, as soon as I finish my round I'll do his pre-discharge check. We'll fill out your blue book so that you have a record to show the early childhood nurse.'

Vivie nodded and Rohan moved on to the next room as if his mind wasn't scheming how to see just what sort of menagerie Abbey had burdened herself with.

In the birthing suite, Abbey had problems of her own. Celia and Eric were becoming more distressed with Celia's lack of progress and the shower hadn't helped as much as they'd all wished.

Celia's baby was descending posteriorly, meaning the baby's spine was lying alongside his mother's spine and the backache was becoming intolerable for the labouring mother. Now Celia's blood pressure was climbing and Abbey was concerned about Celia's previous tendency towards hypertensive disease of pregnancy. Abbey had the feeling there was many hours to go and Celia's reserves were running low after a long night of niggling pains.

'I want an epidural,' Celia panted, and Eric nodded.

Abbey smiled. 'If you feel you need a break from those pains, then I think an epidural is a fair thought,' she said. 'You're over four centimetres dilated and it could be a few hours until you're ready to push. An epidural will give you a rest and relax the lower half of your body enough to help you along. Plus, it will help decrease your blood pressure. If you let it wear off towards the end of labour, you'll still be able to feel where to push.'

She handed Celia the nitrous oxide to breathe in. 'You're doing a great job, Celia. Hang in there. Use this while I go and see Dr Roberts. Hopefully he's still here.'

When she went into the nursery, Vivie was wheeling baby Rohan out of the room. Rohan of the black eyes was laughing with Michelle and he looked up as she approached.

'I want to talk to you,' he said.

Abbey brushed that aside. 'Not at the moment.' She didn't see or didn't care about Rohan's surprise at the abruptness of her answer. 'Can you come and talk to Celia about an epidural, please?'

Back in the labour ward, there was no sign of tension as Abbey and Rohan organised Celia's pain relief. Abbey prepared the sterile set-up of instruments and needles required to position and administer the local anesthetic into Celia's epidural space. Rohan's anaesthetic experience meant they didn't have to wait for another doctor to insert the block and Celia's husband held his wife's hand through the procedure.

Abbey and Rohan worked together with precision to make Celia more comfortable. It was a much-relieved Eric who shut the door after them when they left the birthing suite three quarters of an hour later.

'So now who's making my surgery patients wait?' Rohan quipped as he and Abbey walked up the hallway remarkably at ease with each other.

'All in a good cause,' she said. He was talking about her comment yesterday. It was amazing the way she could follow his thought processes. It was also a bit scary. 'Will I ring you when Celia is ready to have her baby?'

'Please.' He picked up his hat from the desk. 'I'd like to be there if she's pushing with an epidural.'

'OK.' She looked down at the black felt hat in his hand and Abbey shook her head. 'Why do you drag that hat everywhere with you?'

Rohan spun the hat around his finger. 'This is my home. Wherever I lay my hat can be home until I move on.'

Abbey didn't like the sound of that. She'd always been firmly grounded to her home and family. 'Is anywhere home to you?'

He shrugged and pulled his car keys from his pocket. 'I have a house in Sydney and some land back in Tamworth, but nothing that makes me want to stay in either place.'

A coolness insinuated itself between them and Abbey resisted the urge to ask more.

He smiled cynically. 'Well-controlled curiosity, Sister. If you want to know anything more you'll have to be nice to me when I come to the ward.'

Abbey smiled sweetly. 'I'm renowned for my niceness, Doctor.'

'I'll bet,' he said cryptically, and left.

The rest of the day was hectic and Abbey was glad to see the end of the shift. Celia's and Eric's baby was at least an hour off birth so she'd handed over to the afternoon staff. Normally she'd stay the extra time but Abbey wanted to have Vivie and her baby home before the afternoon became too chilly.

By the time she had her new guests settled it was teatime, and to Abbey's surprise and delight Kayla had already prepared a huge bowl of spaghetti Bolognese for everyone, so Abbey didn't have to cook.

It was like having her sisters home again and Abbey revelled in the sense of family that prevailed. Vivie and Kayla had been to the same school and a budding friendship looked likely. They adamantly refused to let Abbey wash up after dinner. Aunt Sophie pronounced the baby her favourite male in the house. It was a happy time in Abbey's kitchen that night.

For Rohan it was solitude in Scott Rainford's empty house, but he couldn't help wondering what was going on over at Abbey's. 'Probably a crying baby, two surly teenagers and a senile aunt,' he said out loud, and then had to laugh at his own moroseness.

It was all none of his business and, knowing Abbey, everything would be running smoothly. She'd be quietly working away in the background to make sure it did. For some ridiculous reason, he worried that she ran herself into the ground looking after all these needy people. A vision of Abbey came to him, tired after work, wiping the perspiration from her brow as she cooked the dinner for her guests, then the wash and clean up as well before falling into bed, exhausted.

The 'falling into bed' bit shifted his mental state from concern to frustration. Simmering frustration and all those thoughts he'd had yesterday came crowding back. If he was honest with himself, he'd like to be the one that Abbey fell into bed with. He'd help take her mind off all these other people. He could be the one to spend a little time on Abbey. If he had Abbey in his bed—he paused and savoured the concept, Abbey of the long legs and soft skin and that curve from her shoulder to her hairline—he'd feel privileged to show her how she deserved to be treated. He'd spoil her so much she'd fall asleep in his arms exhausted for a far better reason than housework.

Rohan shifted uncomfortably in his seat. It must be too long since he'd had a steamy affair. Dalliance and convent Abbey were an unlikely combination and right up there in the realms of fantasy. Platonic friendship was about as far as he'd get with Abbey. Sex aside, maybe he could take her around and introduce her to some of the fun she was missing before he left. The woman deserved a life outside work and philanthropy.

He'd bet she hadn't spent time on herself in years. They could do dinner and dancing and he enjoyed her company. Showing Abbey a good time became a great idea. It beat the hell out of him spending his out-of-work hours alone for the next week or so and it was all in a good cause. The 'Save Abbey from the Doldrums' campaign.

He'd work on it and he'd make sure she didn't get hurt. Even Scott had said he must look after Abbey.

CHAPTER FOUR

'HI, ABBEY. I have a brilliant idea.'

Abbey looked at the dark-eyed mischief glowing from Rohan Roberts's face and mock-shuddered. She continued to fold nappies. 'I really don't think I want to know.'

'You need to take pity on me,' he said. 'Here I am, new in town and hardly knowing a soul. And it's Friday. The most rapport I've established is with a very strict and moralistic nursing sister and I just want to have fun. You have to help me.'

'What on earth are you going on about?' Abbey wasn't sure she approved of his description of her but there was something about Rohan today that shrieked danger and Abbey was quite happy to listen to her inner warning system. 'Cancel that question. What ever it is—I'm not interested.'

He ignored her answer. 'Take me out. Show me the sights.'

He smiled that killer smile and Abbey resisted the urge to cover her heart with her hand to ward off the waves of attraction that were flowing her way. He paced the room and Abbey followed the ripple of well-toned muscles as he moved. No man had the right to be so compelling.

He went on. 'I'm only here for two weeks and we've almost finished one. You're not some young, impressionable girl who will think she's in love with me. We can be friends and do fun things just for the…' He hesitated and changed the word. 'Heck of it.'

Abbey stifled a laugh. 'Gee, thanks. I'm old, un-impressionable, very strict and moralistic.' She tilted her head and continued dryly, 'And you have tickets on yourself. Considering all that, what on earth makes you think that me taking you out would be fun?'

He stopped in front of her and his eyes were suddenly a very different dark, more of slumbering darkness, a darkness that sent tiny shivers down Abbey's back. 'Because, sweet Abbey, you are also strong and valiant and honest and funny. I enjoy your company because you make me feel alive.'

Abbey blinked and the warmth in her face warned her about the sudden colour in her cheeks. She threw down the nappy in her hand and moved away from him towards the window, slid open the latch and let the cool air bathe her back to sanity. The man was like a glass of champagne and she normally didn't drink.

He had no idea how boring she was or what a disappointment she would be. 'Sorry. I'm busy.' She turned back to face him. 'Find someone else to play with. Unlike you, I have responsibilities and I take them seriously.'

'That's right,' he said, and his voice had flattened.

'Too seriously.' Then he shrugged off the darkness and smiled again. 'Think about it, anyway. I'll give you a ring tomorrow morning.'

Abbey's 'Don't bother' was lost in the slam of the front door as he whistled his way down the steps.

Abbey stared after him. What on earth had brought that on? And a voice inside asked what she was missing by refusing to go out with him.

Abbey frowned. She wasn't missing out on anything. She was settled in her life and was busy enough without the need to fit in pleasure jaunts to amuse the transient Dr Roberts.

The insistent ring of the telephone dragged her back to the present and Abbey was glad of the distraction. The casualty department needed a bed, she was told. The rest of the hospital was full and would Abbey take a young woman with a threatened miscarriage?

'If she's happy to come over here, of course I will. Bring her now and I'll have the room ready.'

Abbey turned the bed down in the room furthermost from the nursery, thankful that the babies in there at the moment were reasonably quiet.

When Mary Pace arrived she was pale and tearful and Abbey helped her gently into bed. 'Have you much pain at the moment, Mary?' Abbey asked.

Mary shook her head. 'My stomach cramped all through the night but it's a little better at the moment. I'm so scared I'm going to lose my baby.'

Mary stifled a sob and Abbey squeezed the young

woman's shoulder and handed her a tissue. 'It is scary, and the hard thing is we can't do anything to make it better until your body and your baby make a decision.'

Abbey tucked the girl in. 'Just rest. I know it's hard to try to sleep, but sleep is the best way to make yourself more relaxed.'

Mary nodded and closed her eyes. Abbey tucked the nurse's call button under Mary's pillow and left the door ajar so she could check on her patient without waking her.

She carried Mary's medical notes back to the desk and read what the outpatient doctor had written. It wasn't promising. Bleeding was bad enough, but when it was accompanied by cramps things were looking grim. Abbey remembered it all too well.

At one o'clock that afternoon Mary lost her baby.

Abbey cried with her, then called Rohan. They rang Mary's husband, a truck driver, and he promised to come as soon as he could.

When Rohan came up to check Mary's condition, his sympathy and clear explanations seemed to help Mary who just wanted to go home to her husband.

'As soon as he gets back into town, he can pick you up,' Rohan said. 'Thankfully your bleeding has settled down enough for you not to require an operation as well. Because you've had one miscarriage it doesn't mean you are more likely to have another. Even two miscarriages are still bad luck. Often the reason is because some building block that was needed for the next stage of growth of your baby was missing. Babies can grow until they need the missing ingredient and then they just stop growing.

'It is not your fault. Although we can usually find something to feel guilty about if we try hard enough.' He met Mary's eyes compassionately and she gave a half laugh, half sob.

'I do feel guilty that I may have done too much yesterday,' she said.

He nodded. 'We always do. There was nothing you could do to change the outcome, Mary.'

Abbey had never heard miscarriage explained like that before and she wished someone had said something like that to her.

Rohan went on, 'It's normal to grieve because you *have* lost your baby and all the dreams that went with it. Try not to let anyone upset you when they don't understand your grief. You and your husband know it's real and we know it's real. Abbey will ask the grief counsellor to see you before you leave so that you'll know her personally in case you want to ring her. I'll see you next week so write down any questions you may have in the next few days.' He smiled gently and squeezed Mary's hand. 'Please, don't bottle it up. It's OK to cry.'

Abbey's throat was thick with emotion and she blinked back the tears, wishing that Rohan would finish because if he didn't she'd have to go to the change room and have a big howl herself.

Thankfully, his pager went off, and he glanced at

it before looking back at Mary. 'Anything else you need to know?' Mary shook her head, so he pressed her shoulder and then left for the other side of the hospital.

Abbey sighed with relief.

'He seems a good man.' Mary leaned back and her eyes filled again as the reality of the miscarriage sank into her mind. It was all over. Her baby was gone.

'He is a good doctor,' Abbey agreed. She could see the girl was struggling with her control. 'Do you want to talk or just be alone for a while?'

Mary bit her lip. 'I think I'd like to be alone, thanks, Abbey. I'll ring the bell if I need you. Thank you for being so kind.' Abbey hugged Mary and talked sternly to herself as she walked up the hallway. She did not need to cry about a baby she had lost ten years ago. But that's what she was doing when Rohan found her.

'Abbey?' Rohan came further into the room and closed the change-room door behind him. She looked like a damp swan with her neck bent in a tragic droop. 'Why are you crying?' Normally Rohan would run a mile from this kind of situation because it smacked of getting involved, and getting involved wasn't a part of his life.

But he couldn't leave Abbey like this.

He put his arm around her, not sure if she would push him away, and to his relief she didn't. It actually felt nice to be able to give her some platonic comfort. But she only allowed it for a moment.

'I'm being silly, don't worry about me,' she mumbled into his shirt, then stepped back out of his embrace. She turned her back on him and he heard her blow her nose. There was something ridiculously endearing about her lack of inhibition. Then she sniffed. 'I'll be fine.'

'Is this about Mary's baby or is there some other reason you're so upset?' Rohan hadn't associated Abbey with an excess of emotion so there had to be some reason.

Abbey looked at him and he thought she was going to say it was none of his business. She blinked, and he realised he enjoyed knowing that she was ordering her thoughts when she did that. Then she sighed.

'I miscarried my baby at nine weeks and I never really allowed myself to grieve over the loss. I guess listening to you explain it all to Mary must have pulled the stopper out or something.' She shrugged and stared at a point across the room. She hesitated and then went on. 'It was all a very long time ago. Ten years. I'd been engaged up until a week before I found out I was pregnant and pregnancy was the last thing I needed. I ignored it, didn't tell anyone, and then when I lost the baby the guilt was too much for me. So I shut it all away.' She looked at him again. 'The only person who knew was my doctor, and I'd prefer you didn't tell anyone either.'

Rohan was surprised how privileged Abbey sharing this with him made him feel. He moved slowly so as not to startle her and drew her gently into his arms again. She let him hold her for a moment and he wished he could take her pain away. The sniff of danger that thought left him with made him stiffen. Involvement. He stepped back before she could. 'I'm sorry you had to go through that alone. One day you'll be a wonderful mother.'

Abbey seemed to find that bitterly amusing. 'I'm going to be a wonderful aunt and friend.' She walked over and opened the door. 'And I need to get back to my ward.' She inclined her head towards the exit and Rohan took the hint. 'I'd like to wash my face.' Her voice dropped. 'Thank you for understanding.'

Rohan nodded. 'I'm here if you need to talk.' Then he heard himself say, 'And don't forget I might need you tomorrow.' The residual pain he'd seen in her face reinforced his determination to do something for her.

Platonically, of course. She gave so much to others but, like his mother, she forgot about herself. Abbey needed to have fun and see that life was for living and not just for helping other people to survive their lives. Maybe there was something he could do about that in the time that he had left in Gladstone.

When she went home that afternoon, Abbey wandered into Aunt Sophie's room and sat down.

'Hello, Abbey, love.' Sophie looked up from her races and smiled. 'Got a problem?'

'No, no problem. I just wondered if you thought I

was moralistic and strict and unimpressionable.' She half laughed. 'I know you don't think I'm old.'

Sophie's face turned into a prune with disbelief. 'So who's the moron?'

Abbey laughed out loud this time at her aunt's fierce loyalty. 'He's not a moron. It was the doctor relieving Scott Rainford.'

'Not the Rohan-sigh-Roberts that Vivie's been mooning over?' Sophie pretended to spit. 'If I hear his name again I'll puke in Bella's pot plant.' She looked across at the pumpkin-sized pot beside the window then turned back to Abbey. 'Why would he say something to hurt you?'

Abbey sighed. This was harder to explain than she'd thought and she wished she'd never started it. 'He didn't say it to hurt me.' Sophie made a rude sound then added, 'Moron,' for good measure.

Abbey suppressed a smile. 'Despite all these things he said I was, he also said that I should take him out and show him the sights because it would be fun. He's only in town for two weeks.'

Sophie cut to the chase. 'And you said?'

Abbey shrugged and avoided her aunt's eyes. 'I said I had responsibilities and took them seriously.'

'What? Too many responsibilities to have fun?' Sophie snorted. 'Rubbish. We're all capable of minding ourselves.' She stroked the hairs on her chin. 'Would taking this moron around be fun?'

'Aunt Sophie! He's not a moron and, yes, I imagine

it could be fun if we didn't spend too much time bickering.'

Sophie shrugged and picked up the racing form again.

'So we'll see you Monday.'

Abbey blinked. 'I said no.'

Sophie let the form drop for a moment and glared at her niece over the top of it. 'Good, clean fun—' she punctuated the words with a bony finger '—is just what you need. The next time he asks you, say yes.'

The phone rang at eight o'clock on Saturday morning. Abbey looked at the handset as if it was a snake until she realised if she didn't pick it up the noise would wake everyone in the house. She snatched it up so quickly she nearly dropped the thing. 'Hello?'

'Good morning, Abbey. Were you still in bed?' Rohan's voice seemed deeper than usual and Abbey closed her eyes and wondered what she was doing even considering spending more time in his company. During the long sleepless night she'd regretted telling him about her miscarriage. But she did feel as if her guilt had lightened. Which in itself was a worry if she began to get used to having Rohan to unburden herself to. Scary thought. She'd definitely decided not to go out with him if he asked.

'Hello,' he said again. She hadn't answered him.

'No. I was up. What can I do for you, Rohan?'

She could hear the laughter in his voice and because he couldn't see it she allowed herself a small soft smile. He was such a character.

'A small jaunt to start. This morning I think you should show me the sights and I'll provide the lunch along the way.'

Abbey gave in and sighed loudly into the phone. 'I suppose I can manage this morning, but only because I feel sorry for you. Are we going in your car or Doris?'

'Definitely Doris. After all, you are the host. I'll be at your place in an hour.' Then he hung up.

Abbey looked into the mouthpiece of the phone wryly and then put it back on the hook. It had never taken her an hour to get ready in her life but she quickened her step—just in case!

When Abbey dropped the morning paper with race guides in to her aunt, Sophie quizzed her on the phone call. 'So, was that him on the phone?'

Abbey could feel the smile on her face as she nodded. 'He wants to see the sights and we're going in Doris. I'll be back after lunch.'

'No matter if you're not.' Sophie's eyes twinkled.

As Abbey left the room Sophie called after her, 'And if he wants to drive—let him!'

At exactly nine o'clock the doorbell rang. Abbey took a deep breath and opened the door. Rohan's eyes were laughing at her and to hide the colour in her cheeks she looked down. Bad mistake. Black, hip-hugging jeans covered his powerful thighs and his hat rested in one large hand and shrieked, Virile man ready and waiting.

As her gaze swept up past the buckled belt to his open-necked shirt Abbey couldn't help the tremor of excitement that belied her calm expression. His rugged good looks would stir a woman less impressionable than her and she needed to keep a level head. He was leaving Gladstone soon, she reminded herself.

Rohan waited for Abbey to speak and when she didn't he cleared his throat. He wished it was that easy to clear his mind. Mentally he was fogged by the unexpected picture of Abbey's magnificent hair loose and framing her face. It made her look younger and more vulnerable. Which was a worry. 'Are you ready, then?' he said, and tried not to stare at the modest V-necked pullover that outlined her ample breasts. Why on earth had he always fancied thin women before Abbey?

'I'm ready.' Abbey pulled the door shut behind her and she glanced at his vehicle parked at the kerb. 'Doris is in the garage. Do you want to drive or shall I?' she asked.

The way she looked today, if she drove he'd probably drool all over the seats. 'I'd like to try Doris, if you don't mind.'

Abbey shrugged and he followed her around the side of the big weatherboard house. Everything swayed deliciously when she walked and he wondered if this day out had been a good idea after all.

He felt like a diabetic in a chocolate factory—look but don't touch.

They chugged along the Pacific Highway and surprisingly the silence between them was relaxed, as if they both knew they didn't have to talk. The sun shone brightly over the green paddocks and they drove with the vents open to let in the cool air. Air-conditioning would be a dirty word to Doris, he thought ruefully. When they came to a turn-off she directed him towards South West Rocks and he was glad to get away from the line of traffic Doris had built up behind her. He'd already pulled over twice to let cars past.

'There's an old prison, Trial Bay Gaol—it's a good place to start,' Abbey said. 'It was opened in the late eighteen hundreds and is pretty spectacular, towering over the sea.'

Rohan looked at the rich farming land that edged the river. 'Why would they need a gaol here?'

'It's not used now. The gaol housed convicts to build a breakwater at the entrance of the bay and create a safe harbour for sailing ships on the eastern seaboard. Later on it was used as an internment centre for German prisoners during the First World War.'

'You sound like a tour guide,' he teased.

'And you sound like a tourist,' she teased him back, and they smiled at each other.

'That's what I am' slipped off his tongue, and it was a sobering thought for both of them.

They pulled up in front of the pink and grey granite-block walls of the derelict prison. The fresh sea breeze whipped red strands of hair across Abbey's face so that she pulled a band from her wrist to tie it back. Perhaps it was for the best, he thought, because he so loved her hair free. Then his attention was caught by the pure line of her neck, and his gut softened with unexpected tenderness and he wished she'd take the band out so he could breathe again.

They paid at the gaol office and climbed the old wooden stairs to the museum that eventually led to the grounds on the other side of the tall stone gateway. When they'd examined the museum pieces and old photographs, they wandered through the ruins. Grass grew over the outlines of long-gone buildings. She laughed at his jokes and earnestly explained the quite relaxed conditions the convicts had lived under.

Rohan found his attention straying to watch the expressions chase across her face. Her eyes sparkled and her cheeks glowed and he couldn't believe he'd thought she'd been only pretty when, in fact, any fool could see she was unbelievably beautiful.

They climbed the north-western watchtower and gazed out over the azure sea to the Yarrahappini mountains. Below, on the breakwater, people searched the sea for a sight of the migrant whales that frequented the waters at this time of year.

Abbey ran her hands across the coolness of the knobbly granite and her senses were so heightened she felt she could have drawn the valleys and hills in the rough stone beneath her fingers. The peace and beauty of the scene filled her heart and she sighed with pleasure. Then she turned and rested her back against the parapet, shut her eyes and spread her arms to feel the breeze and the sun in her face.

'Every time I come here I wonder why I don't come more often,' she murmured. She opened her eyes and smiled at Rohan, and he looked so vibrantly handsome that he dazzled her. She shut him out and quickly turned to stare back over the sea.

Rohan slid his arm around her shoulder and pointed. 'Look over there.'

Abbey tried to ignore the warmth seeping into her shoulders from his arm and shielded her eyes to squint in the direction in which he was pointing. 'Can you see a whale?' she said.

Rohan didn't answer but gesticulated wildly with his other hand. People below them looked up at them on the tower and then out to sea as if to find what he'd noticed.

'No.' He grinned mischievously. 'But the people down there think I have.'

She'd known he wasn't to be trusted. Abbey slapped his arm away from her shoulder and tried not to laugh. 'You're terrible.'

Rohan grinned at Abbey's embarrassment and pointed enthusiastically at another section of the bay. More people rushed to the breakwater and stared out into the waves.

'Stop it.' She put her head in her hands, laughing, and shook her head. She could feel her cheeks burn-

ing. 'I'm going down to ground level. You're embar-
rassing.'

'And you look good enough to eat.'

His voice was still playful and Abbey brushed the
compliment away. He didn't mean it but she could
feel his gaze on her as they climbed carefully down
the steep stairway to the ground.

They explored the old cells and kitchen ruins and
Rohan wished he'd brought a camera to capture
Abbey as she stood in the granite archways. Then he
thought of staring at her photo in some new town at
a later date and reviewed that thought. Perhaps it was
better he didn't own a camera.

They went from the gaol to the beach and walked
barefoot halfway around the white sand of Trial Bay
before they turned back. Rohan regaled her with
amusing anecdotes from his student days—nothing
personal, because he needed the distance to stop himself from pulling her into his arms to see if she tasted
as delicious as she looked.

By the time they returned to the car she was wind-
swept and the tip of her nose was pink from the sun
even though he'd lent her his hat soon after they'd
hit the beach.

She fanned herself with the brim and then handed
it back. 'Thanks for that,' she said as she leaned back
against Doris. 'Phew. I'm dying for a cold drink.'

She rubbed her hair with both hands to unflatten it
and her breasts jiggled erotically. Rohan dragged his
eyes away with a mammoth effort.

'We need food and fluids, urgently,' Rohan agreed. And a cold shower, he thought ruefully as he opened the car door for her. 'I saw a kiosk sign on the hill as we came in. Is that any good?'

'Only if you want fabulous food looking out over the bay.' She grinned up at him and her mouth curved invitingly.

He was very close to dropping a kiss on her lips but that wasn't part of the bargain. He shut her door with controlled force instead and lectured himself all the way around the big car.

He was quiet as they drove the short distance to the restaurant and Abbey looked across at him thoughtfully. His short hair was untidily curled from the wind and made him look more like a pirate than a gunslinger, but his tanned face was serious. Something was on his mind. Maybe he was bored now?

She couldn't think of anything she might have said to alter his mood and it had been fun this morning. More than fun. For her it had been a sparkling adventure, and with Rohan by her side everything had seemed brighter and even more beautiful and exciting.

'We can just get a drink if you want to head home earlier,' she suggested, and tried to keep any trace of disappointment from her voice.

He glanced quickly across at her as they pulled up in the restaurant car park. His black brows almost met in the middle and he didn't go to the bother of hiding his disappointment. 'Sick of my company already?'

So he didn't want to go home. Reassured, she denied it. 'Actually, I'm starving! I was being polite. If you're not tired, let's eat.'

He sighed in exaggerated relief. 'Please, don't be polite again, it's been too long since I've had such an appetite. I'm ready to eat the placemats off the table.'

They sat at a table right on the edge of the verandah, under the shade of brown sails, and the sea breeze kept the heat from being oppressive. A sign on the rail said DON'T FEED THE KOOKABURRAS, and Rohan laughed.

They gave their orders and he sat back in his chair. 'Do you come here a lot?' Rohan asked. Abbey gazed over the treetops to the small blue waves in the bay and he watched her face soften at the memories.

'Not for years. My sisters and I used to come here with our parents before they died. It's a great family beach. No rips, shallow water and gentle waves because it's protected.'

'Tell me about your family.' She was such a complex woman if he didn't ask he had the feeling he would learn very little.

Abbey took a sip of her juice and the ice clinked in the glass. Rohan tried not to stare at the moisture left on her bottom lip.

'I have two sisters,' she said. 'Bella is gentle and beautiful, like her name, and is a midwife in a birth centre in Sydney. Kirsten is loud and boisterous and the adventurous one of the three of us. She still has another year in Saudi Arabia before she comes home. I miss them both, dreadfully.'

Rohan tilted his head and suppressed a smile. 'Is Kirsten a midwife, too?'

Abbey smiled and nodded. 'We all are—like Mum was. Mum had a home birth practice and as kids we often went with her. It's in the genes.'

Rohan dipped his head towards her and said in a serious voice, 'Don't tell me your dad was a midwife, too?'

Abbey burst out laughing and Rohan sat back, pleased that he could lighten her mood. 'Dad was a fire chief and before our parents died we did a lot together as a family. Camping, boating, fishing. I can pitch a tent with the best of them. We girls didn't seem to have the sibling rivalry that most families have. Maybe because I was two years older than Bella and four years older than Kirsten, I always felt protective of them. It wouldn't have been fair to fight with them.'

It all sounded so wonderfully different to his childhood. 'I couldn't tie a knot to save myself. I've never camped in my life,' Rohan quipped, and tried not to think of the lonely nights while his mother had worked. Even when she'd been home there'd always seemed to be a lame duck that had needed feeding or clothing or counselling—and not all of them wonderful examples of citizenship—so that his mother had seemed more at work than at home. Until the last one, who had killed her with incompetence.

He shook off the memories and concentrated on a woman who was vibrantly alive. 'Would it upset you to tell me how you lost your parents?' He wanted to know. He didn't know why but he needed to know everything about her and he had the feeling she spent more time listening to others than others listened to her.

She raised her chin as if to be strong in the telling. 'Dad died in a bush fire. The people he went in to save made safety but he was caught in a firestorm. Mum died less than a year later in a car accident, coming home late at night after a birth. Suddenly I was responsible for the family.'

A few sentences and he saw how she had shouldered burdens too great for her years. Her story wasn't that different to his—except that his mother had sacrificed her life for her son and not strangers—but unlike Abbey he'd had all responsibilities removed by the state until he'd been old enough to decide his own future. Maybe that was why she was more giving than he was.

He shrugged off his own demons and tried to imagine Abbey as a young woman, suddenly the only breadwinner in her family. 'You didn't take over your mother's home birth clients?'

Abbey shook her head. 'I was twenty and had only just finished my midwifery. I thought of it, but there just wasn't enough money to support the three of us. Then Aunt Sophie lost her home and moved in as well. So I took permanent work at the hospital and have been there ever since.'

He couldn't help but think, What about Abbey?

Now was the time she should be enjoying herself. She couldn't spend the rest of her life waiting to see if someone else needed her. 'Do you ever want to leave? Now that your sisters have gone? See the world?'

She looked at him as if trying to gauge why he'd asked that question. 'I see the world from where I am. My life is here. I have friends, Aunt Sophie and my sisters have a home whenever they need one.' It was her turn to ask questions.

'What about you, Rohan? Are you ever going to settle down in one place or do you like being foot-loose and fancy-free? What are your goals?'

'My goals?' He shrugged. 'To be self-sufficient and never have to worry about where the next meal is coming from. I wanted to become a doctor, fell into obstetrics because no one seems to want to go that way any more, and I get to see a new piece of Australia every couple of months. I'll never go hungry and could retire tomorrow if I wanted to and still live comfortably.'

It sounded pretty cold and featureless to Abbey. 'What about home and family? Where are your parents?'

His mouth thinned and she mourned the appearance of the protective shell she could see springing up around him. It made him look older and harder than the fun companion of the morning.

There was a bitter overtone to his voice. 'My mother worked herself into an early grave looking after me and every stray loser she could find until she died, and my father could be dead for all I ever knew about him or the help he gave us. They couldn't even find him after my mother died.' His mouth hardened even more.

'Marriage and commitment wasn't there when she needed it. So much for the love she said they'd shared. I used to get wild with my mother when her lost causes took her away from me so I guess I was lucky I didn't have brothers or sisters. I'm too selfish.' He gave a harsh laugh. 'I'm just not cut out for the commitment of home and family like you.'

'Maybe you haven't found the right sort of woman?' Her voice was soft.

His was firm. 'Maybe I'm not the right sort of man!' It wasn't a question.

The food arrived at that moment and both statements went unchallenged.

It was Rohan who broke the silence. 'I'm sorry, Abbey. I have my own demons and shouldn't bring them out on a day like this. In penance I'll pay for lunch.' He smiled and he looked so contrite that Abbey had to smile back. But her heart ached for his insecurities.

'Fine. I'll pay for Doris's fuel. She's nearly as thirsty as we are hungry.' Then she laughed at his frown. 'Don't even think about fighting me on this. You won't win!'

They took the back roads that meandered along the river. Several stops to feed ducks and examine old wares for sale at the side of the road saw their morning rapport fully restored. Perhaps the reasons they were so different were better said, thought Abbey.

It was late afternoon when Rohan turned off the engine of the car back at Abbey's house in Chisholm Road. 'Stay there. I'll open your door for you,' he said, and she sat back as he walked around the car.

It was dark and cool in the garage after the brightness outside and Abbey sat quietly soaking in the memories of the day. When he opened the door he took her hand to help her down off the running board and she felt like Aunt Sophie must have felt fifty years before, getting out of Doris on the arm of her beau.

'Thank you for a lovely day, sweet Abbey,' he said, and as her feet hit the ground he spun her gently so that she ended up in his arms. His kiss was firm and sweet and left an imprint that lingered as if his mouth were still there. Startled, she looked up at him and he tightened his grip to give her a hug. 'I think you're a wonderful tour guide.'

Abbey tried to keep it light. 'And you are a tourist. Don't play those games with me, Rohan, I'll only disappoint you.' She stepped out of his embrace but he caught her hand.

'I don't regret the kiss, Abbey, only its brevity.' He pressed the car keys into her palm and shut her fingers over them before letting go of her hand. 'And I doubt you'd ever disappoint me.'

If she could disappoint a creep like Clayton then someone as obviously experienced as Rohan would surely find her sexual prowess lacking. She laughed harshly and saw his gaze sharpen at the discordant sound. 'Remind me to tell you *that* story one day,' she said, and slipped out of the garage.

CHAPTER FIVE

SUNDAY was quiet until Kayla went into labour. Abbey had tried to prepare her young friend for the tedious length of early labour and reiterated the usual extended time that the contractions would slowly build up over. Of course, it didn't happen like that.

Two nuisance pains at breakfast heralded the start of what was to become one of the shortest labours in history. When Vivie called upstairs to get Abbey from her bed, Kayla's waters had just broken, and without time to throw her dressing-gown on, the girl's moans were floating along the hallway to hurry Abbey's feet.

When she burst into the kitchen, Kayla was gripping the kitchen table with white fingers, and even Aunt Sophie had left her room to find out what all the commotion was about.

'Oh-h-h, oh-h-h, it's coming,' Kayla moaned, and Abbey blinked.

She turned to Vivie. 'Looks like we're having a baby. Ring Dr Roberts because Kayla's baby may still be a couple of weeks early—he's at Dr Rainford's house number. I'll see if I can get Kayla a little more comfortable.'

Abbey rested her arm across the girl's shoulders

and calmed her. 'It's OK, Kayla. Your baby is in a hurry so we'll just manage as we are.'

Aunt Sophie hobbled across with her morning arthritis to the sink and sat a pot of water on the stove. 'Haven't had a birth in this house since you and your sisters were born. Didn't think I'd live to see another one.'

She pulled a plastic tablecloth and some hand towels out of the drawer and handed them to Abbey before making her way towards the lounge for a pillow.

Abbey spread towels over the tablecloth on the floor and urged Kayla into a squat with her hands still holding the table. 'You're doing beautifully, Kayla. Just listen to your body and do what it tells you to do.'

'It's telling me to push and I can't be ready yet. Can I?' She turned anguished eyes towards Abbey who smiled serenely back.

Instinct told Abbey that Kayla had passed the first stage of labour. 'If you're ready, well…you're ready.' Abbey crouched down beside her. 'You'll be fine and baby will be fine. Don't be scared. Just let it happen.'

Sophie was back with some pillows and they made a place for Kayla to lie down if she wanted to. 'I need a dish for the placenta and some scissors and string for the cord, Aunt Sophie.'

'Kettle's on. I'll pop the kitchen scissors and tape in the pot as soon as it's boiled.' The old lady was in her element and Abbey had to smile.

Vivie came back. 'The doctor's coming.'

'Good girl.' Abbey smiled reassuringly. 'Perhaps you could run upstairs and find one of Kayla's rugs for the baby and another towel, then you can hold Kayla's hand because you know more than any of us how she's feeling at the moment.'

Vivie blushed with pleasure at being included and sprinted up the stairs on her errand.

Within five minutes the first bulge of the baby's head could be seen and shortly after the rest of Kayla's baby was born into Abbey's hands with a minimum of fuss. By the time Rohan hurried in, calm had been restored. Kayla was resting quietly with a bonny baby girl in her arms and Abbey, dressed in short pyjamas that exposed miles of legs and cleavage, was just delivering the placenta into an empty ice-cream container.

Rohan smiled at the incongruity of the receptacle and tried to block out all thoughts of yesterday—and a goodbye kiss that had been so sweet it had lingered in his mind all night—to focus on the other people in the room. Aunt Sophie was grinning and Vivie smiled mistily beside Kayla.

'Good morning, ladies,' he said, and his lips twitched. 'What a delightful activity for a Sunday morning.'

'I *don't* think,' muttered Kayla, and everyone laughed, but then she smiled down at the baby in her arms.

'You missed the exciting bit.' Abbey looked up at him, and Rohan spread his hands.

'As usual. You had it all under control, Sister.' He tilted his head in appreciation of her capabilities and they shared a brief wordless rapport before he smiled at the two girls.

'And it looks like Kayla makes beautiful babies like you do, Vivie.' He crouched down beside Kayla and peeked at the baby snuggled next to her. 'Congratulations. She looks closer to term than the ultrasound suggested, and seems happy where she is.' He lifted one pink foot and ran his finger down the baby's sole. 'A few creases there—I'd say she's only about two weeks early.'

The baby started to nuzzle against her mother's breast and they all smiled. 'And hungry already.' Rohan met Abbey's eyes and asked a silent question.

Abbey shook her head. 'No worries. Third stage complete and no stitches needed. We'll come up to the hospital in a while after Kayla has showered and had a chance to pack a bag. That way she can have help while she establishes breastfeeding.'

Aunt Sophie's bright eyes went from one to the other as she watched the communication between Rohan and Abbey with avid interest. 'Do you want a cup of tea, Doctor? Because I sure as heck do.'

Rohan hesitated and Sophie grinned when she saw him glance at Abbey before answering. 'Don't ask her. She'll say she's too busy. Sit with me for a moment while they sort themselves out.' Sophie rose creakily from the chair and put the kettle on again, and Abbey shook her head in mock resignation as she got to her feet.

'This is my Aunt Sophie. Aunt Sophie—Dr Rohan Roberts.' Abbey looked indecisive for a moment and passed the decision to Kayla. 'Would you like a cup of tea, Kayla, or do you want to go into the shower first?'

'Shower, please.' Kayla wriggled uncomfortably under the blanket Abbey had thrown over her and grinned. 'I can't believe how messy one little baby can be!' She hugged her baby closer. 'But she was worth it.'

Abbey smiled. 'As they are.' She glanced at her aunt and Rohan. 'Excuse us.' In a remarkably short space of time, Abbey, Kayla, baby, Vivie and the mess had all disappeared. That left Rohan and Aunt Sophie sipping tea in the kitchen.

Rohan wasn't quite sure where to look or what to talk about. 'Abbey is very efficient,' Rohan said.

'You have no idea,' Sophie drawled in agreement. Then her face wrinkled up and she pinned Rohan with her sharp eyes as if she'd worked herself up to say her piece. 'So what are your intentions with my niece, young man?'

Initially, Rohan had to bite back an impatient rejoinder at Sophie's blatant attempt at intimidation. He stared back at the old lady with her wild hair and wispy chin and her gappy, evil smile—and realised Sophie only cared that her niece didn't get hurt.

How could he complain about that? He agreed.

More people should have been looking out for Abbey and he felt a strange kinship with this funny old lady with her spiky hair and few teeth.

He looked towards the empty doorway through which Abbey had last disappeared, and forced himself to be honest with Sophie and himself. 'I admire Abbey. I enjoy being with her and I don't intend to hurt her. More than that…' he met Sophie's eyes '…I couldn't say.'

'Yet!' Sophie closed her lips after the one word and tapped her teaspoon on the side of her cup. 'That's fair enough.' There was silence for a minute and then Sophie added, 'Just make sure you let me know if your intentions change. Keep it good, clean fun.'

Her voice lowered as if she were talking to herself. 'I won't have her used and hurt like that last cad used her.'

Rohan frowned. 'You mean her ex-fiancé?'

Sophie's attention lifted from the cup she'd been staring into. 'Told you about him, did she?'

Rohan shook his head and wondered how deeply he wanted to become involved in this conversation. 'No. Just that she'd been engaged.'

Sophie huffed in disgust. 'Well, he took her for what she had. Money my sister and her husband had put aside, her young girl's heart and the spark that used to glow when she smiled.' Sophie looked at Rohan with speculation. 'Though I must admit I have seen a glimmer of the old spark lately.'

'Who's an old spark?' Abbey said as she came into the room.

To Rohan's disappointment, Abbey's tiny pyjamas had been replaced by a pair of jeans and a high-necked jumper. He sighed. Still, he had his memories.

'Doris,' said Aunt Sophie as quick as a flash, and Rohan reminded himself never to underestimate the old lady.

Abbey laughed. 'Judging by the bemused expression on our doctor's face, I'd say it wasn't Doris you were talking about, but I'm too busy to worry. Do you know where I put the car keys yesterday? I never lose them and today they seem to have disappeared.'

'Your mind was on another planet when you came home from your day out. Ask the good doctor what happened to them,' Sophie said wickedly, and Rohan decided it was time for him to leave. The women in this house were way too sharp.

He stood up to say goodbye and that brought his eye level above the refrigerator.

'Keys are on top of the fridge, and I'm out of here.' He extended his hand to Sophie. 'It's been interesting meeting you, Sophie.'

Sophie shook his hand firmly. 'You can call me Aunt Sophie. Drop in any time. I get lonely.'

'Between races,' Abbey said dryly, and she smiled at Rohan as she grabbed the keys. 'Thanks for coming.'

He realised that he didn't exist for her at the moment. Just like his mother on a crusade. As a child he'd been jealous but hopefully he'd grown out of that. After she'd died he'd sworn to never be dependent on anyone again, and he wasn't going to start now. Right, then, he thought. 'I'll see you later.' And left without a backward glance.

CHAPTER SIX

ON MONDAY morning life was back to normal. Abbey looked a little tired but was at the desk, waiting to do the round with him. She smiled in a distant way and chatted as they walked down the corridor. Abbey as a distant friend was the sensible thing. Sensible. He was leaving in a little less than a week. She was right—distance was probably the best thing for all concerned. Rohan just wished she'd be a little more distant in his night-time fantasies.

Kayla smiled when they entered the room and Rohan could see the difference from the scared young woman of the previous week. He had to admit it looked like Abbey had done the right thing to take her in. An ironic thought when he'd been so against Abbey's open-house policy and her penchant to fling herself into danger. 'Good morning, clever Kayla.'

He smiled at Kayla and her spiky-haired baby, and leaned over the baby's cot to see what she had named her daughter. He couldn't help the chuckle that escaped. 'Sophia? After Aunt Sophie?'

Abbey shared a smiling glance with Kayla and the girl nodded happily. 'Sophia Abigail. Abbey wouldn't let me call her after her so I've made her middle name Abigail.'

Rohan glanced at the pink in Abbey's cheeks and bit back the teasing comment he'd have liked to have made. Of course, Abbey wouldn't think she'd done anything special, but naming the baby after her aunt would probably give his Abbey more pleasure anyway. His Abbey?

The floor shifted beneath his feet and he glanced up to see if anyone else had noticed a tremor. Nobody mentioned it. He hoped he wasn't falling for Abbey because that sort of internal seismic activity needed urgent attention. Still off balance, he dragged his attention back to the youngest woman in the room.

He cleared his throat. 'So how is Miss Sophia feeding?' He glanced at the feed chart on the baby's cot and his eyes widened. By the amount of times this infant had demanded the breast, Kayla's baby would never starve.

'Like there's no tomorrow,' Abbey said, glad to get away from the naming embarrassment. 'Kayla is managing breastfeeding beautifully and will probably only stay another day before coming home.'

For some reason Abbey was even more aware of the nuances in Rohan's voice this morning and her eyes kept straying to his face as he talked. It was amazing how many times their eyes had met in the short time he'd been on the ward this morning, and she just hoped he hadn't thought she was behaving strangely.

His lashes were long and thick and should have belonged to a girl, but there was nothing feminine about the strong cheekbones and sensual set of his lips. Lips that were firm, yet capable of such sweetness.

She couldn't help the memories of a kiss that had touched and lingered so persistently in her heart that she'd had her sleep ruined for the last two nights. She knew he'd kissed her as a one-off impulse and that he was probably just as disappointed in her kissing skills as Clayton had been.

The phone rang back at the desk and Abbey excused herself to answer it—glad to get away from such a depressing thought. Rohan was just passing through Gladstone and it would take a better woman than her to entice him to stay. She just didn't have the chemistry to be a sultry siren and she never would have. It shouldn't even be worrying her. She sighed and rounded a corner in the corridor just as the phone stopped.

She huffed in exasperation and glanced out the window towards the road, and her stomach sank. Kayla's ex-boyfriend Trevor was limping and weaving up the path and he looked as though he hadn't stopped drinking since the last memorable time Abbey had seen him—or changed his clothes or found his shoes.

Absently, she rubbed the fading bruises on her wrist as she hurried to pass the door before he could open it to come in.

With quick fingers she dialled the supervisor's number and requested security support a.s.a.p.

Abbey stood behind the desk and squared her shoulders for the expected confrontation as the door opened. 'Can I help you?' she asked pleasantly.

Trevor squinted at her as if trying to focus. 'My g'lfrien' had a baby yesterday. Kayla. Where is she?' His slurred voice had the same belligerent tone that Abbey remembered. She kept her voice gentle and non-combative.

'I'm sorry. It's against hospital policy to allow any-one who has been drinking alcohol to enter the patient areas.' She tried a smile. 'If you'd like to come back after you've had a rest, perhaps then you could see her.'

'I know you.' He glared at Abbey. 'You helped her leave me. You broke my toe.' He turned to look out into the street at Doris. 'And that's your car!'

The sinking feeling in Abbey's stomach increased as Trevor's deductive skills functioned much better than Abbey felt they had a right to.

His loud 'I wanna see her now' coincided with the arrival of two burley security guards and Abbey sagged a little against the desk in relief. One of them approached Trevor and shook his hand.

'G'day, mate,' he said as his partner came up on the other side of Trevor. They steered him around and towards the door. 'I see you've been celebrating. Had a new baby, have you?'

'Yeah. And the witch won't let me see it.' Trevor glared at Abbey over his shoulder as they escorted him out the door.

Abbey listened to the guard's friendliness and admired the improvement over the old-fashioned threats. Instead of an ugly scene, it turned into a well-ordered removal. 'Best thing would be to come back later, after you've sobered up. It's pretty special having a kid and you want it to see you looking your best. Don't you?' Their voices faded as they walked Trevor down the steps and Abbey heaved a sigh of relief as she sat down at the desk.

'You didn't come back.' Rohan's voice intruded into her thoughts and she jumped.

He frowned. 'Sorry. Did I startle you?' She looked a little pale. 'You all right?' He was interrupted by the taller security guard.

'He's gone, Sister. Nasty bloke under the weather, that one, but not too bad when he's sober. We've had him before down at the pub. Give us a ring if he comes back.' He smiled at Abbey and Rohan, then strolled off with his friend.

Rohan stared after them. 'What was all that about?'

Abbey was still distracted as she wondered how to break the news to Kayla. There was the added thought of what damage she could expect to be inflicted on Doris the next time Trevor came across her car. 'I called Security to remove Kayla's ex-boyfriend. He was drunk and demanding to see her. It didn't seem a good idea in his state.'

She saw his eyes go to her wrist and unconsciously she covered it. 'Of course it's not a good idea,' Rohan said. 'Did he threaten you?'

Abbey refocussed on Rohan and shook her head. 'No. Though he did recognise my car from when I went with Kayla to pick up her stuff. I called Security when I saw him coming.'

Rohan looked out the window as if trying to see if Trevor was still there. 'I knew this would happen. Why didn't you call me? I was on the ward.'

Just what she needed, a male ego, Abbey thought, and her voice couldn't hide her irritation. 'I can look after my ward without you, Rohan.' Her voice was very clear. 'I'm supposed to ring Security—not the doctor on call.'

Rohan rolled his eyes in disgust. 'I'm not suggesting I was going to tackle him in your hallway, Abbey, but I would have liked to have been beside you while you waited for Security to arrive. You're too independent.'

This conversation was a waste of energy and after two sleepless nights, thanks to him, Abbey didn't have energy to spare. 'Why wouldn't I be independent, Dr Roberts? I'm thirty-one years old and in charge of my own life.'

Now Rohan was irritated. 'And everyone else's life, from what I gather. Maybe you need someone in charge of you to lighten the load, Sister Wilson.'

'Like who?' Abbey said belligerently.

They glared at each other until the ridiculousness of the conversation struck them both at the same time. Abbey blinked and Rohan smiled and held up his hands. 'Truce,' he said, and Abbey nodded.

'I'm sorry, Abbey.' Rohan drew a breath and re-laxed his shoulders. 'You seem to bring out protective instincts I thought I'd finished with,' he said wryly.

'I'm sorry, too. I should say thank you for your concern.' Abbey rubbed her forehead. 'I haven't been sleeping well.' Blast. She hadn't meant to say that. His overactive ego didn't need any further boost.

His look was quizzical. 'And why would that be?'

She said the first thing that came into her head that wasn't the truth. 'Worrying about the girls, I think.'

Rohan's smile disappeared. He'd hoped she'd been thinking of him. 'Stop worrying about people who should be in charge of their own lives. There is more to life than looking after other people's problems, Abbey.'

She smiled at him but there was a hard edge to the tilt of her lips. 'Like not caring? Like being insular and lonely and not accountable to anyone? Like you?'

Rohan frowned at the sharp stab of discomfort he felt at Abbey's reading of his character. He was shocked that was how she saw him and he wondered how much truth there was in her words. 'I'm not lonely, and being unaccountable also means no one has to worry about me either. And I have no need to interfere in other people's lives to feel fulfilled.'

Abbey snorted and he couldn't help think she sounded like Aunt Sophie. 'Well, you don't seem to have much problem sticking your oar in my business.'

She laughed, unamused, and the sound grated on his ears. Something was eating at her and her usual calmness had disappeared. He noticed the dark circles under her eyes and his mounting anger disappeared.

His voice gentled. 'Where did all this come from?' Her eyes shone with unshed tears and her answer was something he least expected.

'You shouldn't have kissed me.' She clapped a hand over her mouth and almost bolted down the corridor. Her guard was down for once and he took off after her. She'd clamp down and he'd never find out why if he didn't get his questions in before she erected that wall again. He followed her into the change room and leant his back against the door to block the exit.

'Why shouldn't I have kissed you, Abbey?' His voice was gentle but demanded an answer, and she turned slowly to face him. He thought it was too late and she wasn't going to reply but then she gave another one of those bitter little laughs that he'd be glad never to hear again from Abbey.

Her voice was low and he could tell she was striving to keep it steady and impersonal. 'Because you made me wish I had the skills to be a real woman. I'm hopelessly frigid. Now, leave me alone!' The last three words were hissed between clenched teeth as she pushed past him to open the door.

He dug his shoulder into the door and blocked her attempt to escape.

'Just a minute. Who told you that?'

She winced at his persistence and raised her head. 'The only man who would know.' She pulled the doorhandle again and it rattled against him. 'Now, let me out of here.'

Rohan was trying to fathom how she could have gained such a ridiculous idea and he didn't budge. 'The ex-fiancé? He said you weren't a real woman?'

Abbey whipped around and faced him. Her eyes were incandescent with anger and he thought she'd never looked more beautiful. Beautiful—but he was glad there wasn't a weapon in the small room or he'd be dead on the floor.

'Do you mind?' She glowered and slapped the door. 'If you don't open this door, I'll scream and Michelle will open it for me.'

He stepped back but his words followed her as she left. 'You're a flesh-and-blood woman all right, and I can prove it to you.'

Rohan followed Abbey up the hall and Michelle popped her head out of the nursery. 'What's going on out here?'

'Abbey couldn't open the change-room door.' He consoled himself with the half-truth and kept going.

Abbey was in the corner of her office, typing away like an enraged woodpecker at the computer, and he hesitated as he looked in. He didn't want to leave her like this but she probably needed some space after the last few minutes. His brain was still reeling.

'I'll be in my rooms if you want me.' He spoke to her back. She didn't answer and he couldn't help his parting comment. 'I bet it was his fault and not yours.'

Abbey heard his footsteps walk away and her fingers slowed and then stilled. Where on earth was her brain when that man was around? She couldn't believe she'd blurted those things out. Things she hadn't told a soul about in ten years, and she'd handed them to him on a platter. Maybe she should take a week's holiday until Scott came back because she doubted whether she'd be able to see Rohan Roberts without blushing for a long time.

Unfortunately, she didn't have that leeway. Five minutes later Abbey heard the door open and the unmistakable sound of a woman in labour. She rose to her feet and met Michelle at the desk as the nurse responded to the same sense of urgency as Abbey.

Abbey's first impression of the woman's abdomen size made her accept that Rohan probably needed to be there.

'Grab the wheelchair, please, Michelle.' She took the bag the blonde woman was carrying and glanced up the hallway to see if anyone else was with her as Michelle pushed the wheelchair up behind her and helped the woman into the chair.

'Have you booked in yet?' Preprepared admission notes could be invaluable here.

'No. My name is Kerriann Sears and my husband is overseas with his work.' Big blue eyes looked at Abbey for reassurance. 'My baby isn't due yet.'

Michelle pushed the wheelchair into the birthing suite and Abbey tried to get as much information as she could before the next contraction. 'I'm Abbey and this is Michelle. How many weeks pregnant are you, Kerriann?' Abbey flipped the cover off the bed and plumped up the pillows.

Kerriann stepped out of the chair and carefully across to the bed before her face grimaced with the next contraction as she lay down. 'Thirty-two weeks on Thursday,' she panted. 'This is my first baby. Is this labour?'

'Looks like it to me.' Abbey nodded sympathetically and held the young woman's hand while she breathed through the contraction. 'What time did this start?' Abbey asked and glanced at the clock.

'I've had pains in my back since last night but these pains in the front came about an hour ago and they're really close now.' Kerriann winced as another contraction started.

Abbey nodded at Michelle. 'Get Rohan on his mobile. We might catch him before he leaves his car. I want him back here. Tell him Kerriann is thirty-one plus weeks and in established labour. I'll put an intravenous line in if you do a delivery set-up just in case.'

Abbey pulled her IV trolley across to the bed. 'Have your waters broken, Kerriann?'

'No, but I do have some pressure down there.' Abbey weighed up the risks of a vaginal examination with the disadvantages of waiting until Rohan came. 'We'll just hope your cervix hasn't started to open yet and will spare us some time to give you drugs to help turn off the contractions. I'll need to put a drip

in your arm so we can give you medications as we
need to.'

Kerriann nodded and Abbey applied the tourniquet
and felt for a vein. 'Doctor has only just left and will
be back in a couple of minutes.'

Kerriann bit her lip. 'What if I'm ready to have my
baby before the doctor comes and the drugs start to
work?'

Abbey understood her fear. 'I don't think you are,
but if baby is that close we can only catch him or her
anyway. Sometimes they're just determined to come.
Ideally, we'd like to at least slow your labour for
twenty-four hours so that baby could have some cor-
tisone to help mature his or her little lungs before they
have to start breathing.'

Abbey went on. 'Thirty-one or thirty-two weeks is
early but most early babies are fine for the first hour
and that's enough time for us to get the neonatal ex-
perts here. Most little ones that age do really well but
there may be more than a few weeks of ups and
downs in a bigger hospital than this before you can
take your baby home.'

Rohan arrived and Abbey felt her face stiffen as he
glanced around the room and then at Abbey. 'Hello,
everyone.' His eyes twinkled at Abbey's frozen look.
'Did you miss me?' Abbey stared expressionlessly
back and Michelle grinned, oblivious to the undercurrents. Rohan didn't wait for an answer.

He moved across to the bed to Kerriann and his
voice softened. 'Hi. I'm Dr Roberts. I hear your baby

is impatient to meet you.' Abbey pulled the sheet
down to expose Kerriann's abdomen for Rohan to do
a palpation to establish the position of the baby.

'Well, at least your baby is coming head first.' He
smiled at Kerriann. 'A lot of babies come bottom first
at this stage of pregnancy.' He took the gloves from
Abbey for the internal examination. 'Let's see where
you're up to.'

Nobody spoke until after Rohan had finished and
removed his gloves. He sat on the edge of the bed
and took Kerriann's hand in his to provide what comfort he could.

'You're four centimetres or nearly half-dilated so
you'll have your baby some time soon.' Abbey and
Michelle exchanged a glance. 'Which means we
won't be able to stop your labour, but we'll try to
slow it down and get you to a bigger hospital before
baby is born.'

His voice lowered. 'Scientists haven't been able to
make a humidicrib as good as your uterus and that's
the best way to transport tiny babies.' He smiled and
Kerriann tremulously smiled back.

'There is a special retrieval team called the new-
born emergency transfer service that comes up from
Newcastle or Sydney if the air ambulance can't get
you down there before you deliver. We'll just have
to wait and see how much time we have as we get
things organised.'

He stood up and nodded in approval at the IV line
ready to start. 'We'll put up the Ventolin to try and

slow the contractions and give the first dose of
Celestone Chronodose intramuscularly to mature
baby's lungs and hope for at least twelve hours'
grace.'

He looked at Abbey. 'I'll get on to NETS if you
can try the air ambulance.'

Kerriann's eyes were filled with fear and the shine
of tears, and Abbey could see she was overwhelmed
by the situation she found herself in. What a horrible
time for her husband to be away.

Abbey felt so sorry for her as she loaded the IV
flask with the Ventolin and commenced the infusion.
'This medication may make your heart race and you'll
feel a bit shaky, too.'

She drew up the Celestone. 'Plus…' she waved the
syringe '…I need to give you an injection in your
bottom now to help mature your baby's lungs. Is that
OK? This medication encourages your baby's lungs
to produce a substance called surfactant that stops his
or her lungs from sticking together and makes them
function better when they have to work.'

'OK but I hate needles.' Kerriann cringed.

'So do I,' said Abbey cheerfully, and Kerriann
smiled reluctantly as she rolled over.

When Kerriann was comfortable again, Abbey
asked, 'Are your parents somewhere close that they
can come to be with you?' Kerriann needed someone
of her own to be with her and Abbey was happy to
ring anyone.

'My mother lives at Willstown but I haven't seen

her since she married her second husband last year. He's a horrible man. I keep telling her to leave him.'

Abbey frowned at the undercurrents in her patient's voice. 'Would you like Michelle to ring her or even give you the phone so you can talk to her?'

Kerriann bit her lip. 'We could try but he probably won't let her come and she always does what he tells her.'

Abbey nodded at Michelle. 'We'll just have to figure out a way to get her here. Michelle is pretty good at diplomacy.' Michelle came across and sat where Rohan had been and Abbey squeezed Kerriann's hand. 'I have to nip out to the desk to make some phone calls to organise your transfer to Newcastle and Michelle will use this phone and try and wangle your mum here for you.'

Kerriann bit her lip and nodded. 'I hope so.'

Abbey leaned closer to Michelle. 'Be as devious as you have to, Michelle. Use my name if you want or anything else you think might help. She needs her mum.'

During the next hour Kerriann's labour slowed a little with the drugs, which was lucky because it took that long to arrange for the air ambulance and liaison between the two hospitals. Rohan was able to be fairly confident that she'd be safely transferred to Newcastle before her baby was born.

Kerriann's mother only just made it before the air ambulance crew landed and Michelle, who went with Kerriann and Rohan to the airport, said it was worth the effort and cajolery to see the two women draw strength from each other for even that short a time.

When Rohan and Michelle came back from the airport, Rohan looked at Abbey several times as if he wanted to say something, but he held his peace. Abbey heaved a sigh of relief when he was paged to the other side of the hospital.

Abbey surveyed the disarray of the equipment left over from the morning. At least she had something to take her mind off her discussion with Rohan as she and Michelle cleaned up, she thought, and then remembered Trevor. She'd put off speaking to Kayla about her visitor because Abbey herself had been in no fit state to talk to anyone after the discussion in the change room.

Reluctantly she set off down the hallway to see Kayla and she hoped the girl wouldn't consider a life with her baby's father.

When she entered the side ward, Kayla had her back against the wall with her baby in her arms. Somehow Trevor had sneaked in. He'd caged Kayla in, with a hand on either side of her head on the wall so that she couldn't get away. Kayla was crying.

Abbey's anger at such bullying blocked any rational thought for her own safety. 'What do you think you're doing?' Abbey's voice was like a whiplash and Trevor jumped and spun around.

His eyes stared at Abbey with unblinking ferocity and his head wobbled from side to side with menace.

'Back off, lady,' he snarled. 'This is none of your business. I already have a score to settle with you.'

Abbey refused to be cowed, though she could feel the shudder of fear creeping around the edges of her control. Trevor looked to be under the influence of more than alcohol and to try and reason with him would be useless. She felt for the cardiac arrest alarm beside the doorframe and mentally shrugged at the confusion it was going to cause on the other side of the hospital when she pressed it.

Firmly, Abbey's fingers depressed the button and the alarm light outside Kayla's room door flashed on and off in time with the monotone buzz that echoed throughout the hospital in one second pulses.

She didn't care if the whole hospital came with a cardiac arrest trolley as long as they could get Kayla away from this madman. Abbey hoped he didn't know what the sound was.

'Leave this ward at once, Trevor,' she said, and took a step towards him to keep his attention on her.

He left Kayla and her baby to swagger menacingly across the room towards Abbey. Abbey flicked a glance at Kayla and inclined her head to encourage the girl to shift well out of his range.

Kayla nodded and slowly slid her bottom along the wall towards her bed, clutching her baby against her breast.

Trevor narrowed his eyes and curled his lip. 'And what if I don't?'

A chill of fear trickled down Abbey's back and she

hoped the cavalry would hurry, but she held his look unflinchingly. 'Then you'll be thrown out.'

'You and whose army? What if I don't let you out of this room?' he taunted, just as the bottom door of Maternity was flung open and the thunder of almost a dozen pairs of feet ran down the corridor.

Abbey stepped back into the hallway in front of them and called, 'In here.'

The look on Trevor's face almost brought a smile to Abbey's mouth as Rohan, in front of two other doctors, six nurses and two wardsmen, surged into the room.

Rohan headed straight for Abbey and she nodded that she was all right.

'It's more of a house arrest than a cardiac arrest but thanks for coming, everyone.' She pointed at Trevor. 'This man is a threat to my patient and he's refused to leave.'

Rohan and the wardsmen backed Trevor into a corner until he cowered into a chair.

'We do all kinds of arrests,' Rohan said, and though his voice was light the steel in his eyes had cowed braver men than Trevor. He went to the nearest phone, spoke into it briefly, and came back to Abbey. 'The police will be here in a few minutes.' He looked again at Trevor and then sat on a spare chair. 'We'll wait.'

After the police had taken Trevor, Rohan had to return to the other side of the hospital, but he promised to return as soon as he could.

Abbey sat on the bed with Kayla. 'You will have to do something more official to keep him away, Kayla.'

Kayla's face was white with distress and Abbey hugged her.

'I know,' Kayla said. 'The policeman has begun an apprehended violence order for me and it's time Trevor left us alone for good.' She looked at Abbey. 'I'm sorry it happened here, Abbey.'

Abbey shrugged. 'This is a much better place for it to happen than when you're somewhere on your own or even at home. Sometimes things work out for the best.'

'Would it be too much trouble if I went home with you this afternoon instead of tomorrow? I feel really well, it's not as if I had a long labour to get over or anything.' Kayla's voice was diffident and Abbey couldn't blame her for wanting to leave the hospital.

'That's fine. Rohan hasn't checked Sophia yet but he can do that when you're at home. I finish at three so you have plenty of time to get organised. I'll ring Aunt Sophie and let them know.'

Later, after fielding a dictatorial phone call from Rohan about ensuring her safety and retelling the story at afternoon handover, Abbey was glad to take Kayla and Sophia and head for home.

She had to admit that the rest of the morning had put her own embarrassment back in perspective. Mortification because of what she'd told Rohan was nothing compared to what Kerriann and Kayla had to worry about.

Abbey decided to put her previous conversation with Rohan out of her mind. Hopefully, he would forget it, too.

CHAPTER SEVEN

WHEN Rohan knocked on Abbey's door just after seven that night, he remembered she hadn't been sleeping well. Hopefully, she hadn't taken herself off to bed early.

Since his mother had died, he hadn't put himself out to help someone just for the sake of helping, but he would never forget Abbey if he abandoned her in this state. Well, that was the story he'd told himself as he'd prepared to come over.

It really was beyond his comprehension that Abbey believed she would always disappoint a man sexually, and her fears still had him shaking his head. For someone so confident in every other area, Abbey vulnerable about her femininity was something no one would have guessed.

Rohan knew he wasn't the man for her, he wasn't worthy of her, but if he could make her see how wonderful she was and how much she had to offer the man who did deserve her love, then he'd have achieved one worthwhile thing while he'd been here. And he enjoyed the time he spent with Abbey.

When the door opened, Abbey looked more weary than he'd ever seen her. She grimaced and for a minute there he wondered if she'd slam the door in his face.

She sighed. 'Hello, Rohan.'

It wasn't the most enthusiastic greeting he'd ever had but he'd take it.

'Hi, Abbey.' He held up a bottle of champagne and a punnet of strawberries. 'Peace offering. I'm sorry I bullied you today in the change room.' She didn't say anything and he tried again. 'Apart from which, it was a pretty huge day and I'd like to share a drink with you.'

She sighed again but stepped back to allow him to enter. He looked around the large hallway with doors leading off it and a staircase that curved up to the next floor's landing. He hadn't taken much notice when he'd come the day that Kayla's baby had been born and the house was larger than he'd thought. To his surprise, apart from the drone of horse-racing commentary in the distance, there was no one about.

'Come through into my study. You can join Clive and me in front of the fire,' Abbey said.

Rohan felt like slapping himself on the forehead. Of course she'd have some male friends. He mentally shrugged away his unreasonable disappointment and entered the room to find it empty as well—except for a large German shepherd that rose on his haunches and bared his not-inconsiderable teeth as Rohan came into the room.

'Sit, Clive,' Abbey said as she lifted a pile of nursing magazines off the only other chair in front of the fire. 'Sit, Dr Roberts,' she said with a mocking smile, and Rohan and Clive both sat. 'I'll get two glasses and a dish for the strawberries.'

When she left the room, Rohan looked around. It was a feminine but friendly room, book-lined with an old oak desk and an even older oak chaise longue with colourful cushions under the window. A huge framed Gordon Rossiter painting showed a purple sunset over what had to be the mountain range he could see in the distance, and he stood up to have a closer look. Clive growled and the dog's hackles rose.

Rohan wasn't a dog person. 'It's OK, Clive. I'm just going to look at the painting.' When he took another step away from the chair, Clive bared his teeth and leaned with even more menace towards Rohan, as if daring him to move again.

'What's your problem, mutt?' Rohan tried a placatory smile but Clive remained unimpressed. His mistress had said, 'Sit.' He growled until Rohan edged back to his seat. Satisfied, Clive folded himself back to wait in front of the fire and continued his sentry duty on the intruder.

When Abbey came back into the room, Rohan stood up and so did Clive with a snarl. Abbey frowned at the dog and put her tray down. 'I see you two have been getting acquainted. Play nice, boys.'

Rohan reached across slowly and started to unfasten the foil on the champagne. 'Your dog seems to think I'm not to be trusted.'

Abbey smiled blandly. 'German shepherds are supposed to be a very intelligent breed.' When he didn't rise to the bait, she went on, 'So, what brings you here tonight, Rohan?'

Rohan started carefully. 'In regard to our discussion earlier today, I think I may have a solution to your problem.'

Abbey raised her eyebrows. 'I would have said it was more harassment than a discussion, but go on if you really have to. I'm intrigued what problem you seem to think I have.' She spoke softly but there was an edge of warning to her voice.

Rohan poured two glasses of champagne, popped a strawberry in each and then handed her a glass. 'Perhaps we should drink a toast first.'

Still sceptical, Abbey raised her glass. 'Need a hit of alcohol under my belt first, do I?'

He pretended to ignore her comment and went straight to diversion. 'To Sophia Abigail and her house full of aunts.'

Abbey blinked. 'I'll drink to that.' He could see she was trying to work out where he was going with this and he bit back a smile. She took a sip and started to put the glass down, but he forestalled her with his hand.

'And to young Rohan and his house full of aunts.'

Abbey sipped again and he could tell she found the taste a little more pleasant this time. Perfect. He may just live to finish this conversation.

Rohan continued, 'To Doris, who is the most interesting car I have ever driven—and the slowest.'

Abbey had to smile at that and she obediently sipped.

Rohan sipped as well to hide his satisfaction. 'And Aunt Sophie, who is the most determined old lady I've met in a long while.' Abbey sipped.

'And last of all to Abbey Wilson, who is my new friend and a warm and generous person who doesn't trust me an inch but for whom I have a proposition.'

The glass stilled against Abbey's lips. 'What proposition?'

There was a challenge in his eyes as he said, 'You have to drink to that before I tell you.'

She drained the glass and set it firmly on the table. 'I'm listening...' Abbey raised her own eyebrows in a return challenge. 'And so is Clive.'

Rohan couldn't prevent a quick glance at the dog whose ears had pricked up at the mention of his name. Yellow eyes met black and neither blinked.

Rohan shrugged and accepted the challenge. He set his glass down and smiled at Abbey. 'I have a solution to help you gain a little experience with a man.'

'I don't want experience with a man,' she said flatly. The words were stark and shone as if in neon lights in front of her, and he knew he had to be careful.

'I'm not talking about seduction here, I'm just talking about the lead-up. A little light-hearted practice to take away the awkwardness.' Rohan had known this would be hard to explain and Abbey looked ready to set her dog on him. He approached it from a different angle.

'Look, Abbey, I believe you're a warm and sensual woman who's had a bad experience. You say you're not a real woman and that you're cold as far as sex is concerned. That's absolute garbage. Let me help you so that when *the* man comes along, the one who can promise you the stars, you'll be ready for him.'

Abbey shook her head in disbelief. 'I can't believe you're saying this. You have an ego the size of a house. That has to be the sleaziest con line to get a woman to bed that I have heard in my life.'

Rohan sat forward on the chair towards her and his eyes were earnest as he tried to will her to consider his words. 'Not to bed, Abbey. Just to the bedroom door. You say you haven't had experience with men and you've let that creep stunt you for ten years. If I thought I could convince you, just by *telling* you that's how it is, I would. But that's not going to work. You've taken his words in too deep.'

His voice became a little self-mocking. 'I have some experience with women.' Abbey grimaced in distaste and he shook his head. 'Think about it as similar to what you do for Vivie and Kayla. You take them away from a bad experience and you nurture them until they can learn to face the world, expecting to be treated right. Knowing they are worthwhile people who deserve respect.

'Let me accustom you to someone wanting to nurture you until you can see you're an incredibly warm and sensual woman who any man would be privileged to take to bed. I'm leaving in a week or so and you'll never have to see me again.'

Abbey couldn't believe what she was hearing, and he was still talking. Each word was like a knife, stabbing her in her belly, because if he'd known she was attracted to him he'd never have said any of this.

Oblivious, Rohan went on. 'We don't have long but that works for good and bad. Practise on me. I can teach you to be comfortable with your own sensuality. No strings. No future embarrassment. Think about it.'

No strings, Abbey thought painfully and picked up her refilled glass to hide the glimmer of tears in her eyes. What about the strings you've woven around my heart already and you've only been here a week? What about the emptiness that I'll be left with when you leave? What about *after* you've taught me how much I really do need to feel a man's arms around me? Think about it, he says. Ha!

The scariest part of this whole conversation was the tiny part of her that was screaming out for her to say yes. The wanton part of Abbey ached to feel Rohan's arms around her and his lips against hers. Who else in the world would she like to discover the delights of physical closeness with than Rohan?

Abbey shook her head vehemently. 'I did think about it and you're mad. You'd better leave before I ask Clive to show you out.'

'Let's go back a step.' Rohan was at his most persuasive. 'We do enjoy each other's company.' He met her eyes. 'Don't we?'

She thought of that magical day at South West Rocks and the conversations they'd had. She thought of the tingling anticipation she couldn't help in the morning as she waited for him to start his round and the verbal sparring they engaged in after he arrived. Yes, she enjoyed his company, and it wasn't as if she could contemplate 'practising' with someone she didn't enjoy being with. But since when had she considered practising anyway?

She narrowed her eyes at him and finally nodded agreement with his last sentence. 'I enjoy your company—but that doesn't mean I would enjoy becoming more intimate with you!' She just hoped her nose hadn't grown like Pinocchio's with that last whopper.

She saw some of the tension ease from his shoulders and realised that he'd at least been nervous about asking her. It made her feel a little better that the discomfort wasn't all on her side.

He continued, 'I respect you, Abbey, and I don't want to do anything to endanger our working relationship or our friendship.'

'So you say.' She conceded that reluctantly.

He smiled and she had no defence against his smile. She could feel the beginnings of her resistance soften and melt like a candle in the sun.

He took her hand and she didn't pull away. 'All I ask is that you relax when you're around me, and if

I show some affection you can return it and not lose any sleep over it.'

She shook her head but she knew he could tell she was almost considering the idea despite her initial reluctance.

How was she supposed to cope with this conversation? Her voice was uncharacteristically melancholy. 'I realise you feel sorry for me but what made you think I'd agree to this?'

His eyes softened. 'I'm not offering this out of pity. I'm offering it in friendship.' He squeezed her hand and she felt the heat travel up her arm.

'And I'm not suggesting we do anything you don't want me to. But, Abbey, ten years is a long time to hold the wrong idea about yourself. You don't have to prove anything to me—I'm proving it to you. We'll have fun.'

Her eyes clouded. 'I hope the cure isn't worse than the disease.'

'I stop any time you say.' He let her go and raised his glass and Abbey realised he'd refilled her glass, too. 'To educating Abbey.'

She sipped slowly and her smile was wary. 'We'll see. But you have to learn as well. You can come to dinner tomorrow night and see why I enjoy my time with the people I live with. Are you willing to try that?'

What did he have in Scott's empty house that was better than the opportunity to spend more time with

Abbey, even with others present? It was an unequal battle. 'I think I can manage that.'

Clive had gone to sleep. Abbey stood up and Clive opened one eye before he returned to his snoring. 'I need to think about this strange proposition of yours, and I certainly don't need any more bubbles.' She could feel the glow in her cheeks and admitted to herself she might not have responded as calmly to his proposition if she hadn't had the wine to dull her reservations. 'I'll put a stopper in this bottle and we can finish it tomorrow after tea.'

Rohan stood as well. 'You're the boss.'

Abbey tilted her head sceptically. 'Why does that not ring true?'

'Oh, ye of little faith.' He smiled and the mischief that she had no defence against was in his voice. 'Walk me to the door, sweet Abbey.'

When he stood on the step and the darkness was behind him, Abbey laid her hand over her stomach protectively to still the flutter of nerves.

She knew he was going to kiss her and her fear of disappointing him warred with nervous anticipation to feel his lips on hers again. Maybe she was normal because she certainly didn't feel repulsed like she'd been every time Clayton had tried to kiss her.

Rohan put his hands on each side of her cheeks and turned her face towards his. 'Goodnight, Abbey,' he whispered as his lips descended on hers, and Abbey forced herself to relax between his hands.

Firmly yet with aching tenderness his mouth

touched hers, and she could taste the tang of champagne and smell the sweetness of strawberries. He
brushed her lips with his own until heat trailed across
her skin, leaving delicious sensations that didn't make
her want him to stop. Funny, that.

Warm fingertips stroked her cheeks, then behind
her ears and finally they slid with purpose until he
held the back of her head in his strong hands. All the
while Rohan brushed her lips with his until Abbey
tilted her face to catch him as she searched in return
for something she didn't recognise. She felt him smile
with delight against her and she smiled, too, in wordless agreement.

Then his mouth settled on hers more firmly and all
laughter was gone as he leaned into her and she loved
the feel of his strength against her. His hands came
down to capture her hips and pull her against him.
Abbey stiffened and his hands soothed her until she
could feel the rightness of the sensations he was gen-
erating. There was no doubt that he was also enjoying
the first lesson.

Finally, with gentle persuasion, he parted her lips
and ever so slightly touched her tongue with his own.
Abbey felt the jolt right down to her toes as if suddenly her whole body was coated in heat. He deepened the kiss until she was drowning in the sensations
that Rohan generated just by the warmth of his breath
and the barest sensation of his tongue against hers.
Slowly he circled and stroked and stirred coals of de-
sire that frightened her with vibrant intensity. When

she didn't repulse him he stroked deeper and suddenly it was as if Abbey had always waited to dance this dance.

She couldn't be passive any more and her first electric movement drew a groan from Rohan that sent spears of primitive satisfaction through Abbey and drove her to be bolder. The dance became a heated tango and the eroticism of it ignited fires in her breasts and low down in her stomach as she swayed backwards and forwards against his chest. His hips dug into hers with a rightness that was frightening yet exhilarating.

Before she could quite grasp the feelings he'd generated, he receded until only their lips touched. His lower lip brushed up and down over hers and their breath mingled and the great ache grew in the region of Abbey's heart. It was beautiful and tragic and addictive and all the things she'd been scared it would be. They stood together and he gently kissed her face until his strong arms gathered her close and she buried her head in his shoulder to hide the tumultuous emotions he'd so easily aroused.

They stood quietly for several minutes like that. It seemed that neither of them wanted to break the spell, and Abbey could hear his heart thumping and the raggedness of her own breath wasn't that far from the unevenness of his. Finally he stepped back and stared into her eyes.

He brushed one cheek with his fingertip. 'Goodnight, sweet Abbey,' he said again, and she watched him walk down the path without looking back.

When she shut the door her hand was shaking against the latch. This was a bad idea.

Rohan drew a deep lungful of cool air as he walked back to Scott's house. His heart still pounded from the sensation of Abbey's body against him and he couldn't believe the emotions that consumed him. This wasn't lust or a two-week stand.

He'd fallen in love with Abbey Wilson.

One decent kiss was all it had taken and he knew it wasn't just sex—because he'd walked away.

Walked when all he'd wanted to do was claim her as his, spend all night kissing and loving her. And when the sun came up and he could see the light in her eyes, he would take her again, slowly, gently, and make her infinitely his.

His?

Who was he to heal the wounds left by that other man when he wasn't much better?

How long could he stay in one town, with one woman, and not feel trapped by the tendrils of responsibility that came with the territory? And of all women, he'd fallen for one who would expect the same generosity of spirit that was such an integral part of her.

Not only expect it but deserve it, and he wasn't of her calibre.

He didn't want the whole commitment and more.

His idea of utopia didn't include the demands of children, extended family, lawn-mowing on Sundays and constantly supporting those less fortunate. He knew what it was like to come second to other people's needs and long ago he'd accepted he didn't have enough moral fibre to cope with the feelings of resentment he'd relive with a life partner.

So he'd done the sensible thing. Decided against marriage. He especially wouldn't let Abbey down like that.

And he should never have offered to show her the road to her own sensuality because now that he knew that he loved her that path was strewn with danger for both of them. He needed to rescind that offer. What he needed to do was stop kissing her.

The next day, Rohan was quiet at the ward round in the morning and Abbey pondered the unexpected development as she drove home.

Once she'd got over the shock of the passion Rohan had stirred in her, she'd actually begun to believe that Rohan must be right. She had felt fabulous and even powerful towards the end of their time out on the step, and maybe it hadn't been her fault that sex with Clayton had been so unpleasant.

When she thought about it, the true Clayton had proved very disagreeable, so the sex couldn't have got any better.

She couldn't believe how liberated she felt just thinking about sex. She'd missed the young adult fumblings and practice that she assumed most girls managed to acquire before they settled down to marriage. After Clayton had belittled her, she'd refused to even think about her own worth sexually.

Abbey felt the warmth in her cheeks and she stifled a grin. Of course the eye-poppingly erotic dream she'd had last night had helped as well. Rohan would have been anything but quiet if he'd known what he'd done to her last night in her bed, and everywhere else for that matter.

She couldn't believe she'd subconsciously acquired such explicit sexual knowledge. She felt like the weight of a hundred years had dropped off her and she would always be grateful to Rohan for that.

'You look like the cat that ate the cream.' Sophie hobbled out of the kitchen and poked a bony finger at Abbey.

'I had a good day at work.' Abbey peered around Sophie into the kitchen where Vivie and Kayla were working. 'What's going on in there?'

'They're making a cake for your Dr Roberts. Is he still coming for dinner?'

Abbey nodded. 'He said he was. I think I'll go have a shower.'

Sophie laid her hand on Abbey's arm. 'There's more news. Bella's coming home, tonight or tomorrow. She said if she gets too tired driving, she'll stop at a motel for the night.' Abbey's delight was infectious and Sophie smiled with her.

'Fabulous,' Abbey said. 'I can't wait to see her. Did she mention how long she was staying?'

Sophie shook her head sagely. 'She didn't say much but I wouldn't be surprised if she was home for a while.'

Abbey frowned at the note of concern in Sophie's voice but she just nodded and climbed the stairs to her room. Bella's on-off relationship with an obstetrician in Sydney hadn't been smooth, but she would tell Abbey when she was ready.

Rohan pushed the doorbell at six-thirty and Abbey opened the screen with a smile that warmed him at the same time as it tore his heart with the knowledge of certain loss.

'Hi, Rohan. Come in.' She stood back to allow him to enter and he could see she was bubbling. He didn't think he'd seen her so happy. He brushed her cheek with his lips as he went past because he couldn't resist it. The look she gave him was old-fashioned and made him smile.

'You seem very pleased to see me or is there another reason you look like you've won the lottery?'

She grinned up at him and he felt like taking her face in his hands and losing himself in another one of those earth-shaking kisses he hadn't been able to get out of his mind.

'My sister's coming tonight or tomorrow. I'm so looking forward to seeing her.'

Rohan came back to earth and his ego winced. She

was excited about someone else. Get used to it, he taunted himself, and searched his memory for the conversation they'd had about her family. 'That would be Bella, from Sydney—am I right?'

Abbey stopped and gave him a measuring look. There was a wry tinge to his voice that she didn't understand and wasn't sure she liked. 'Yes. Thank you for remembering her name.'

'I have a very, very good memory.' His eyes darkened and the unmistakable innuendo sent a shiver down Abbey's back. She couldn't help but blush and when he slid an arm around her waist and ushered her in front of him, thoughts of Bella were pushed behind the feel of him against her.

She definitely wasn't frigid. Abbey hugged the thought to herself. Rohan's fingers brushed her neck and she shivered. She could hear the smile in his voice when he said, 'I won't tease you any more.'

She twisted back to look at him and pouted with mock disappointment. 'And I was just getting used to it.'

He rolled his eyes as she laughed up at him. 'From nun to *femme fatale* in one day. Quick learner.'

Abbey thought of the dreams she'd had and she moved ahead of him into the kitchen as her blush deepened. 'You have no idea!'

Rohan would have liked to have followed that train of thought but they'd found the rest of the 'family' and he stifled his irritation at having to be pleasant to the people who shared Abbey.

The kitchen table was set for five and Sophie was rocking in a wicker rocker near the window with a baby in her lap.

Kayla was shelling peas with another infant draped across her knees and Vivie was stirring a big black pot on the stove with some delicious aroma making its way out of the saucepan and across the room to Rohan. Despite the fact there were six souls more than he normally had around him at dinner, the room was calm.

The adults looked up and smiled and the warmth and serenity seeped into that place he kept separate— the place that reminded him he'd never be a family man—and put a sliver of 'maybe' where there'd only ever been a 'never'.

Abbey walked ahead and lifted a squirming young Sophia Abigail off her mother's legs and snuggled the infant into her own neck. The baby grizzled but didn't cry. 'What's your problem, chicken?'

The sight of Abbey and Kayla's baby sent a shaft of paternal phobia through Rohan's heart. Abbey looked like a red-haired Madonna and it caused a physical pain to think of her with another man's baby. He wasn't ready to think about this. Luckily, the room carried on without him. Kayla shrugged at Abbey. 'She's got the fidgets.'

Abbey turned slowly and indicated that Rohan should find a seat at the table. 'Let's give her to Rohan while I help you guys.'

Sophie snorted from her chair. 'Why not? He's got

a way with women.' Rohan narrowed his eyes at the evil witch in the corner and she cackled back.

Rohan took the baby girl and she snuggled into his arms as if she belonged there. With tiny head jerks, she nudged her cheek against his chest a couple of times and then suddenly she was asleep. Rohan looked up to share the moment, but the person he wanted to show was busy.

He watched Abbey for the next twenty minutes as she prepared some rice and laughed with the girls and sparred with Aunt Sophie. Still she managed to meet his eyes every now and then to share a secret smile. Her generosity of spirit awed him and he wished he could be all that she deserved because maybe he could get used to this. But if he did get used to it, something would happen and it would all be snatched away anyway. Better not to expect miracles.

Dinner was noisy and fun and delicious, and to his surprise the girls shooed Abbey into her study with him and commandeered the washing-up.

Rohan brought along the leftover champagne from the night before and the mood was desultory and pleasant.

She'd moved the chaise longue in front of the fire so they could sit together. 'I see you've moved the furniture,' he said as he followed her into the study. He couldn't help teasing her and she blushed, as he'd known she would.

'I'm always moving furniture,' she said, and he hid his smile as he sat down beside her.

'I really enjoyed the meal tonight. Thank you for asking me, Abbey.'

She smiled and relaxed beside him. 'I'm glad. I know it's different to what you're used to, but different can be good.'

He shrugged and met her eyes. 'I'll never be a family man, but I can appreciate what others can see in it.'

Abbey reached out and touched his cheek, something she wouldn't have done twenty-four hours ago, and the warmth that flooded through her made her see that she loved him. It wasn't a blinding revelation— just a sureness that said it was no mistake and had happened. She loved him in a hundred ways and loved him so much she knew she had to let him go.

And now that she knew she loved him, it was going to be a hundred times more painful to see him leave. But let him go she must. Why would a man with his lifestyle want to exchange it to be tied to a woman like her? They were so different. She was family orientated and he was self-sufficient.

She would always appreciate that he had woken her from the isolation in which she'd locked herself, she knew, but it was only going to hurt more if she didn't accept that there was no future for them as a couple. Abbey swallowed the painful lump in her throat.

He needed to see he was free. 'Nobody expects anything from you, Rohan. I appreciate your friendship and maybe one day, somewhere, you'll find a place that feels like home to you.'

Apparently it was all right for him to think those things but Rohan didn't seem to appreciate hearing Abbey say it. 'Don't patronise me. I'm not one of your lame ducks, Abbey,' he snapped. 'I've managed to stand on my own two feet for more than twenty years. You don't have to save me.'

Abbey grasped the opportunity she knew she had to take for her own sanity and plastered a smile on her face. She pretended to ignore his ill humour. 'I'm glad you said that—because you don't have to save me either. I'd like to call off the lessons you had planned for my ''education''!'

He pulled back away from her as if that had been the last thing he'd expected her to say to him. 'Was it that bad?'

She punched his arm gently to lighten the mood. 'You know it was great.' Toe-curlingly great and—now that she knew she loved him—far too dangerous. But she wasn't going to say that.

She met his gaze squarely. 'I've been running myself down for too long. You were right—you proved it to me with one kiss. It was Clayton and not me. I have to thank you for that. So I don't need lessons. I think we both understand each other a bit better and I'd really rather not talk about it any more.'

He opened his mouth and then shut it again. There was a mutual awareness of the shift in their relationship. Last night's kiss had changed everything and if they weren't careful things could become complicated. He shrugged and reluctantly abandoned the topic.

Her voice was determinedly bright. 'So where do you go from here when your time is up?'

'I might go back to Tamworth for a while but I'm not sure.' He didn't want to think about the time when he was going to leave Abbey for ever. 'Tell me about your sister who's coming tomorrow. Tell me about Bella.'

CHAPTER EIGHT

BELLA WILSON was tired. She'd assisted with a long labour the day before and with her disastrous love life she was mentally exhausted as well as physically weary.

It had been dark for an hour and the road was starting to blur in her headlights. She knew she had to stop but she was so frustratingly close to home!

STOP, REVIVE, SURVIVE, the flashing road sign warned her and she took it as an omen. A minute later one of those road traffic authority commercials came on her radio and the announcer droned, 'Most accidents on country roads occur within an hour from home.'

'OK, OK. I hear you,' she grumbled, as she came into Willstown. She'd have dinner and some coffee at the Star Hotel and hopefully she'd wake up enough and wouldn't have to stay the night. She knew if she rang Abbey, her sister would come and get her, but Aunt Sophie had said Abbey's doctor friend was coming for tea. The last thing Bella needed to do was be nice to another doctor.

Bella bypassed the noisy front bar and entered through the side door directly into the bistro. She'd been here once or twice with her friends before she'd

134

moved to Sydney and knew the food was good. Quiet music played in the background and the Bay Marie was full of steaming pastas that made her mouth water.

'Good evening, madam. May I help you?' The bistro supervisor's voice was smooth and a touch too friendly.

His face tugged at a long-buried memory but that really wasn't surprising when she was so close to home. Bella was too tired to worry and ordered coffee and pasta. If she didn't feel a whole heap better after that, she ought to stay the night.

She watched him serve the pasta and tried to pin down where she'd seen him before, but her brain was foggy. She just didn't care enough. 'Do you have any rooms vacant in case I'm too tired to go on?'

'Certainly, madam. There's three left, and breakfast is included. If you decide to stay, I'll show you what's available after your meal.'

Bella nodded and took the cutlery he handed her over to her table. A group of teenage boys came in at the same time as her pasta arrived and the room became noisier, to the detriment of her vague headache.

The seafood pasta was delicious but her head had started to thump and she wondered where her coffee was. 'I think I'll have a look at the rooms, then I'll decide.'

'Certainly, madam.' The man's smile was kind of oily and Bella stamped down the feeling of unease she felt in his presence. She was being paranoid. He probably had a wife and six kids. He was old enough.

He reached behind the bar and collected a bunch of keys before leading the way up the wooden stair-case to the accommodation section. The whole area was clean and old-fashioned and remarkably quiet. He unlocked a room at the end of the corridor and stood back. Bella walked into the room and it was small but homey, and the flowered quilt on the bed and fluffy bath towels looked so inviting she decided to stay.

'This is fine. I'll take it. I'll slip out to my car and get my things.'

She followed him down to the bistro again and filled out the registration and paid for the night. She didn't notice the narrowing of his eyes as he saw her surname.

'Perhaps you'd like your coffee up in the room, where it's not so noisy?'

'Great idea.' He wasn't so bad. He gave her a key and turned away to make her coffee and Bella forgot about him.

But he didn't forget about her. He glanced up to see if anyone was watching and then reached into his pocket for a small plastic ampoule and snapped off the top. He squeezed the contents into her cup.

Rohan was on the ward the next morning when Abbey took the telephone call from Sophie.

'What do you mean, something is wrong with her?

Is she sick, hurt, upset?' Then the blood drained from Abbey's face and she sank into the chair beside the desk. He moved over to stand beside her because she went so pale he thought she was going to faint right off the chair.

'Has she rung the police? No. I'll be home as soon as they can find a replacement. Give her my love.' She put the phone down slowly and turned to face him.

'Bella is home.' Her voice shook. 'She was drugged and Aunt Sophie says Bella thinks she was attacked last night at the Star in Willstown. She can't remember anything after she went to bed, but woke up this morning…' Abbey stopped and bit her knuckles and then picked up the phone to call the supervisor. 'I have to go to her.' When Abbey had briefly explained, the supervisor promised to come over immediately and relieve Abbey until she could get someone else in.

Abbey's eyes filled with tears. 'Why Bella? She's so gentle and sweet.'

'Why anyone?' Rohan enfolded her in a loose embrace. He wished he could have protected her from this distress. Without thought, he kissed the top of her head and then realised what he'd done.

He stepped away and tried to distance himself by being practical. 'I know it will be hard to ask Bella but she needs evidence to put who ever did this to her in a place where he can't hurt other people.'

Abbey flinched and then nodded, and quietly

Rohan went on. 'She needs to have blood taken to screen for drugs still in her system. It's less than twenty-four hours so there will still be traces. She'll need the results later. And swabs.'

Abbey straightened her shoulders as the supervisor came into view. 'Will you come back with me?'

Rohan forgot he didn't get involved in other people's lives. Abbey needed him and he couldn't hesitate. 'Of course.'

By the time Abbey had Bella tucked up in bed, and the police had been, Rohan needed to go back to work. His receptionist had done well to reschedule the morning session of patients in Scott's rooms, but to catch up was going to be a nightmare. Abbey had been so upset when the police had said they'd drawn a blank on Bella's attacker, he'd hung around, worried she was going to do something stupid to find the man.

The bistro supervisor had an unbreakable alibi for his time after work, the young men had seen nothing suspicious and no one had seen anyone else loitering who could have been responsible for Bella's attack.

Bella hadn't spoken much and as the hours had gone on she'd spoken less and less. Rohan could see Abbey was beside herself with worry and he'd stayed at the Chisholm Road house despite there not being much he could do.

He caught her as she hurried towards Bella's room. 'I have to get back to work, Abbey.' She blinked and he wondered what was going on inside her head. If he could have protected her from all this, he would gladly have done anything.

He tried reassurance. 'They'll catch him, Abbey.'

'When?' Her voice was bitter.

Rohan winced. 'As soon as they can. You've done every thing you could to help, now leave it all in the hands of the police.'

He saw the wall come up between them as soon as he said it and he sighed. 'I'll come back tonight, and I'll bring a sedative in case Bella wants one.' He leaned towards her to drop a kiss on her forehead but she stepped back out of reach. He stared at her for a moment but she didn't say anything.

Abbey watched Rohan leave and she knew she'd been hard on him. For a man who wasn't into domestic crises he'd been a wonderful support. But she was going mad with the inactivity of the police. She wanted to see the attacker found and put away before his next victim suffered and—to be honest—Abbey wanted to avenge her sister. The last time she'd seen Bella she'd had trouble containing her own tears and all this procrastination was not helping.

Over the next few days Bella became more and more withdrawn. The drug test had proved a measured dose of the sedative had still been in her bloodstream the day after the attack. All they had to do was capture the man.

Bella barely spoke to anyone and Rohan had suggested to Abbey that Bella consider a short course of antidepressants to help lift her over the shock, but her sister had refused. He'd been coming over every night, and his good humour had done much to keep the entire household from sinking into depression.

Vivie had been the real heroine as she'd voluntarily relived her own experience for the police to help with their enquiries. Vivie was the only person Bella would talk to and Abbey was at her wits' end.

When after a few days they were still no closer to finding the culprit, Abbey knew she had to do something. Finally she'd had enough waiting. She found her aunt in her sitting room in front of an unusually blank TV.

'Bella said the bistro supervisor was familiar. I know the police say he couldn't have done it, but it's the only lead. If I could see who he is, I think we'll find our answer. I don't know when I'll be back,' she told Sophie, 'but I can't sit around here doing nothing any more.'

Sophie didn't look surprised. 'Have you told Rohan you're going?'

'It has nothing to do with him. He said to leave it all in the police's hands but Bella needs this resolved now.'

Sophie nodded and didn't even try to change her niece's mind. Abbey had always dealt with the family crises. 'Be careful.'

Abbey pulled up at the Star Hotel and sat in the car for a few minutes to steel herself to go in. It was still light and when she entered the bistro there was no one behind the bar. She stifled a disappointment that was unreasonable. It wouldn't be that easy.

A small, timid woman came out from the staff area and smiled. 'Can I help you?'

Abbey offered a token smile back and pretended to cover a yawn. 'Some dinner and a room, please, if you've got one. I don't think I can drive any further today.'

'We've plenty of rooms. Did you want to see one?'

Abbey shook her head. 'No. I've stayed here before.'

The woman looked at Abbey again and Abbey could tell she was trying to place her. All she said was, 'Driven a long way, have you?'

'Yes,' Abbey was noncommittal. 'I'll have the quiche and salad, thanks. And a coffee.' She handed over the money, wrote the address of her training hospital and her mother's maiden name and gestured to the nearest table. 'I'll slip out and get my overnight bag from the car. Won't be long.'

When Abbey came back her meal was waiting on the table with a steaming cup of coffee that Abbey couldn't touch. By the time she'd forced down a meal she didn't want, she still hadn't seen any male employees and was beginning to think she'd wasted her time. Then the staff door opened and a tall man carried through a carton of wine to put behind the bar.

Inexplicably, her heart thumped and something told her this was what she'd come to find out. She tried not to obviously stare but she couldn't see his face behind the box and her breath caught when she almost managed a glimpse of his eyes in the mirror on the wall behind him. Suddenly, instead of putting the box down, he changed his mind and carried it back out again.

Abbey frowned and tried to pin down a flicker of recognition that dragged at her memory, something about the set of his shoulders and neck. If only she could have seen his face.

Despite a shiver of foreboding, Abbey stood up and took a step to follow him when a hand fell on her shoulder and spun her around. She bit back her gasp and it was Rohan who spoke first.

'What the hell do you think you're doing?' If she thought she'd seen Rohan upset the day he'd seen the marks on her wrist, it had been nothing to this. He'd obviously worked himself up into a fine rage on the car trip over and his grip on her arm was fierce and unforgiving.

Abbey shook her hair out of her face, and glared at him. Her heart was still thumping with the fright he'd given her. 'Don't swear at me. How did you find me?'

'You would drive a saint to cursing,' he ground out in an undertone, but he didn't answer the question. He didn't need to. She'd have something to say to Aunt Sophie when she got home.

He shook her slightly. 'We're leaving, Abbey.

Before you get hurt or do something that jeopardises the whole investigation.'

She tried to free her arm but he didn't let go. 'This is none of your business, Rohan.' She looked down to where his fingers still gripped her arm. 'Let me go. Now,' she snarled.

Rohan loosened his grip and ran his hand through his hair in frustration. His voice remained low and intense and he glanced around to check that no one could overhear. 'What is wrong with you? I'll follow you home and we'll discuss it. This is not the right way to go about this.'

Abbey rubbed her arm. 'The right way is taking too long and the wrong way is jeopardising nobody but myself. I want my sister's attacker behind bars.'

'Well, your aunt might think you're capable of saving the world, and you may think no risk is too great, but I'm not going to stand by and see you end up worse than your sister.'

Abbey threw her head back and glared at him. 'You have no say over what I do, Rohan Roberts. Go away, before you spoil everything.'

He crossed his arms across his chest. 'No. I'm not leaving.' He stood there like a great oak tree in the middle of a paddock and just as movable.

Abbey felt like grinding her teeth in frustration. She wished he would just disappear and let her get on with what she'd set out to do. She closed her eyes and took several deep breaths. When she opened her eyes again Rohan was standing in the same spot. Maddeningly, he waved, as if to say, I'm still here.

It was useless. She'd never achieve anything with him around. She'd have to come back another time. 'Smart alec,' she snapped.

'Dumb Abbey,' he shot back, and there was no humour in his voice.

She frowned and tried to glare at him, but his response had been too idiotic. She shook her head with an unwilling smile and some of the purpose drained from her. Abbey turned away from him to reorganise her plans and she had to admit, at least to herself, a tiny part of her was glad to leave. She'd had a really bad feeling since she'd caught a glimpse of that man. Now she had to extricate herself from the hotel without drawing too much attention because she really didn't want to endanger the case for the police.

Rohan followed her in his car as she drove home and his headlights shone on her face via her rear-view mirror. It was as if his presence illuminated the changes in her life since she'd met him.

When she thought about it, nobody had enforced their will on her for a very long time and she really didn't understand why she was heading home when it was the last thing she wanted to do.

Maddeningly, she couldn't even tell him what she thought of him in private, because when she got home there'd be people everywhere. Without thought she flicked on her indicator and pulled Doris over to the side of the road.

Rohan's Range Rover stopped about a centimetre from Doris's rear bumper. He switched his lights off and Abbey was plunged into darkness. The sudden silence and absence of light would have been eerie but Rohan climbed out and was at Abbey's door in about two seconds flat.

'Now what are you doing?' he growled, and when he saw she intended to get out he opened her door and Abbey stepped out to face him.

Doris's interior light threw a shaft of light across his face and she glared up at him. 'Stop trying to run my life, Rohan.'

'Well, stop trying to endanger yourself.' His eyes blazed as he thought about what could have happened to Abbey. 'You could have been attacked yourself.'

She shrugged. 'Sometimes you have to take a risk. If the worst came to the worst I would still survive. I have been attacked before.' The words disappeared into the darkness around them and her shoulders slumped. Her voice lowered. 'That's why I can't stand by and let Bella know that whoever did it is still walking around.'

Rohan's froze. 'Who attacked you and when?'

Abbey sighed. 'It was a long time ago and Clive helped me fight him off. I reported it and he ended up in gaol because he'd already been on a bond. I know, as a victim, it preys on your mind that they'll come back if they're not caught. I want to save Bella that, at least.'

Rohan shook his head and swallowed the nausea

in his throat that rose when he thought of Abbey in danger. 'Let me stay at your house until this is all over. It will ease Bella's mind. I won't let anything happen to anyone in your family, Abbey, but you have to promise me you won't do anything stupid to put yourself in danger.'

Loving him as she did, the thought of Rohan under her roof, all night, every night, was too much. She was having enough trouble sleeping as it was.

'No.' She couldn't. 'I don't want you staying. Let me handle this.'

Rohan drew a frustrated breath. He knew it was hopeless to try and change her mind tonight. 'Then remember I'm only a phone call away.'

She nodded and climbed back into her car. He followed her all the way home and sat in the street with his engine running until she'd safely let herself into the house.

Later that night, a dispirited Abbey had gone to bed and Sophie sat and worried over her two nieces as she watched the reruns of her races. Unusually, Clive started to bark outside.

Sophie moved awkwardly over to the window. 'Quiet, Clive. You'll wake the house.' Clive started to growl and bark and Sophie frowned. She pushed up the window to peer towards the garage but couldn't see any movement.

'Anyone there?' Her voice quavered as she leaned out the window. She heard the sound of Abbey's upstairs window opening above her head and glanced up.

At that moment someone rose from the garden beneath her window and knocked her back into the room with a rough hand, before sprinting off into the darkness. Sophie tumbled backwards and landed on her bottom, knocking her face on the side table as she went down.

Stunned for a minute, she couldn't believe what had just happened. 'Stupid old cow,' she muttered to herself as she turned over onto all fours and dragged herself up onto her lounge just as Abbey burst into the room.

Her dishevelled aunt was grumbling and shaking and Abbey rushed across to help her sit up. 'Are you all right, Aunt Sophie?'

'I'll be fine,' she said impatiently. 'My pride's hurt, along with my rear end, but I'd like to know what whoever it was were doing out there.'

Abbey traced the red area on Sophie's face where she'd knocked the table, and her aunt winced. She'd need some ice.

'Did you see who it was?' she asked her aunt, hoping that Sophie had got a better look than she had.

'No, darn it. I was looking up at your window and he pushed me back into the room so he could run away. Cheeky pig.'

'Thank goodness you're all right. But I think you'll have a black eye tomorrow from that knock.'

Sophie cackled, a tad shakily, but Abbey admired

her composure. 'Reckon it will ruin my looks?' Abbey smiled and slid her arm around her aunt and hugged her.

'You're always beautiful to me.'

Sophie snorted. Despite the quiver in her voice, her humour still seemed intact. 'Kid, you need to get out more.'

Abbey went over to the window and shone her torch around the yard. 'If you'll be all right for a couple of minutes, I'm going to see what happened in the garage. I'll be back in a moment with some ice for your cheek.'

This time Sophie wasn't so sure. 'Maybe you should ring the police or Rohan.'

Abbey looked back over her shoulder as she left the room. 'If I'm not back in a few minutes, you do that. Rohan should have a look at that eye of yours anyway.'

Abbey eased open the back door. Clive rushed up to greet her and she ruffled his brown and grey fur. 'Hello, old mate. You're a good boy, barking at the bad man.' Clive glued himself to Abbey's legs and she walked with more confidence across to the garage and switched on the light.

At first she didn't notice anything amiss, but when Clive sniffed and then growled at Doris's tyres she could see the damage. Each tyre was flat at the base and when she shone the torch closely, slash marks were clearly visible. Abbey sighed and looked at Clive. 'A bit more effort needed, mate, if you didn't find him until after he'd done this.' As if ashamed, Clive dropped his head and then rolled his eyes up to look at Abbey until she patted him again.

'OK. So he was really quiet. Looks like we've got an enemy now, Clive. You'll have to stay on your toes. All we have to find out is whether he's an enemy from before Bella's attack or after. Or if the two are connected.'

Nothing else looked disturbed so Abbey turned off the lights and went back to have a quick look under Sophie's window to see if she could see any signs of the intruder's presence. She shone the torch across the garden bed soil and her heart skipped when she saw that directly under Aunt Sophie's window was one large footprint. It was a footprint, not a shoeprint, with the intruder's toes clearly outlined. Abbey sighed. At least she knew who the intruder had been, unless there had been a sudden increase in the amount of shoeless people she'd gained as enemies recently.

She shone the torch across the upper windows, from her window across to Bella's above the steps and then Vivie's and Kayla's. There was no way anyone could climb up there so she'd just have to keep the front and back doors locked. Satisfied, she turned towards the house but didn't see Rohan arrive.

Rohan couldn't believe she was walking around in the dark with just her dog and a torch for protection. When Sophie had called he'd felt sick at what could happen to Abbey and her family, and he hated the taste of that fear. He'd never worried about his own safety and hadn't been aware enough to worry about his mother's mortality until it had been too late. But the fear he felt as circumstances seemed to be closing in at Abbey's house was frightening the life out of him.

'What are you doing outside?' His words were louder than he'd intended and when she jumped and spun to face him he lowered his voice. 'Don't you have any sense?'

She flared at him, 'You're responsible for giving me more heart attacks than anyone else, the way you've been creeping up on me over the last few days.' She rubbed her forehead irritably. 'For goodness' sake, Clive was with me and there's no one here now. Though they've done a good job on slashing all of poor old Doris's tyres.'

Rohan bit back what he wanted to say. Slashing tyres wasn't easy, and someone had to have felt pretty strongly to go to the bother of doing all four. 'I'm not even going to get involved in how you know there's no one here now.'

She shone her torch back at the garden bed. 'I think I know who this was, anyway.' She explained about Trevor and his bare feet and Rohan fought back the urge to say he'd told her so about taking Kayla in. Because he wasn't sure if he'd be right.

After the last few days, he couldn't wish that Kayla and her baby weren't safe with Abbey, rather than at risk with the abusive Trevor. So many things were changing that he didn't know where he stood any more. They agreed not to mention their suspicions to the others yet to spare Kayla's feelings. Abbey would mention it to the police in the morning.

Rohan followed Abbey inside and they went through to Sophie's room. To Abbey's surprise, Bella was out of bed and she'd found some ice for her aunt's cheek.

Rohan moved across to the old lady and gently turned her cheek. 'What happened to you, old thing?'

'I'll "old thing" you, whippersnapper. I smacked my cheek and took a tumble onto my rear end.' Sophie lowered one gnarled hand under the edge of her bottom and rubbed it.

Rohan bit back a smile. He put his hand out for the torch that Abbey still carried and checked Sophie's pupils. When he was satisfied he handed it back to Abbey before crouching back down beside the old lady.

'We'll get an X ray tomorrow though if you can sit on it, you're probably in for bruises on your bottom at the worst.' He smiled at Bella who was hovering anxiously over her aunt. 'The ice will help her cheek and eye a lot, Bella. Good job. Though I'd say tomorrow she'll have a shiner.'

Bella nodded jerkily. 'Do you think whoever it was will come back?' Bella looked over her shoulder at the window and her nerves were showing.

'I don't think so, but I'll stay the night in Abbey's study if no one minds, just in case.'

Sophie and Bella nodded enthusiastically but

Abbey was less so. What was she going to do when everyone became dependent on Rohan to save them—and then he rode off into the distance? It had to be soon. All very well for him to be the macho hero, but she'd have to be the support mechanism when he'd gone. It would be better to stand alone now than have to grow into it all again after he left.

'Don't bother.' Her voice was loud in a sudden silence. 'I'll sleep downstairs.' Her female relatives looked at her as if she'd grown another head, and Rohan's expression didn't change.

Before Sophie or Bella could say anything, Rohan stepped up to Abbey and nudged her towards the door.

'Abbey and I are just going to have a little chat in the study. Maybe you ladies should think about a cup of tea before you go to bed to settle your nerves.' Sophie shut her mouth with a snap and Bella nodded. After glancing at her aunt, she disappeared towards the kitchen.

Abbey sighed and led the way into her study where she threw herself onto the lounge and rested her head in her hands. Everything seemed to be spiralling out of control. It was emotionally draining and she was just so tired. Rohan sank down beside her and his hand lowered to rest on the back of her bowed head, then slid down onto her neck to gently knead the taut muscles beneath his fingers. Abbey stiffened for a moment and then gave up any resistance to his soothing touch.

'You don't have to do this alone, Abbey. I'm here.'

Her reply was muffled but he heard the words. 'But not for long.'

'Actually, Scott rang today and he's coming back tomorrow.' Abbey sat up and his hand fell away.

She crossed her arms across her chest to steel herself to hear the words. 'That's exactly what I mean. Relying on you is a waste of time.'

Rohan put his hand on her shoulder. 'I told him I want to stay on for a while and he's happy to share the workload.'

Abbey turned her head to look at him, unable to believe what he'd just said. 'Why would you decide to stay in Gladstone?'

He smoothed her cheek. 'Why do you think?'

This was too important and she didn't want to look like a fool. 'I don't have the energy for games, Rohan. Suppose you tell me.'

He started to rub her neck again but she was too tense to relax and she brushed his hand away as she waited for his answer.

'Until they catch this person who's harassing you and your family, I can't leave. I'd never rest, not knowing that you were all safe.'

Abbey choked back her bitter disappointment but she couldn't trust herself to say anything. Her expectations had been ridiculously high. Rohan was a good friend but he was never going to be more than that. He just didn't have it in him to give.

Weariness descended on her like a heavy cloak and

even her head felt too heavy to hold up. 'There are blankets and pillows in that camphor-wood chest over there, Rohan. Stay if you want to. I'm going to bed. I'll see you in the morning.'

He could hear the exhaustion in her voice. 'I'll drop you at work on my way home, then. I'll bring some things over tomorrow because I'm not leaving until this whole business is resolved. I imagine it will take a while to replace the tyres on your car.'

Abbey rubbed her forehead. 'I'd forgotten about that. Fine. Whatever. Or maybe I'll take Bella's car. I'll look in on Aunt Sophie and then go to bed. Goodnight.'

Abbey checked on her aunt but Sophie sent her on her way. Bella had already gone up. Abbey knew she should stop in and see her sister but she really couldn't cope with more at the moment after Rohan's announcement.

How long did he plan on staying and how on earth was she going to keep him at arm's length when all she wanted to do was bury her head against his chest? She was tired and she was scared and she hadn't been able to keep her family safe without him.

Then the next problem would be when he did leave. She was frightened by how much she was going to miss him now that she'd admitted she'd fallen in love with him. And seeing him every day and at work and here in the evenings for the last week. Despite their concern over Bella he'd always seemed to organise that hour before he went home with just the two of them in her study, and that hour had been an oasis in an emotionally turbulent time.

She'd seen the effort he'd made to adapt to being part of their household. The way he'd even managed to stay in Sophie's good graces, which was no mean feat for a man. He'd been kind to the girls and excellent with the babies. She sighed. Maybe his time with them would stand him in good stead one day but it was going to break her heart when he left.

CHAPTER NINE

ROHAN pulled the blankets and pillow from the chest and threw them on the lounge. He'd left the door to the hallway open so he could hear any suspicious noises. It was quiet and he stood for a moment and looked at the short bed and the curved end. It was a great lounge for snuggling up to Abbey but would be hopeless to sleep on. He dragged the blankets onto the floor. He just hoped Clive hadn't left any fleas behind.

The floor was hard but he had more on his mind than comfort. He could still see the disappointment on Abbey's face when she'd asked why he was staying and wished he could have given Abbey what she'd hoped to hear. But he didn't have it in him. As soon as he could guarantee she was safe, he would leave. He wasn't good enough for her and never would be, and he was doing neither of them any good by prolonging the agony.

With Scott home to take back his workload, he himself would have more time to work on finding out who was stalking Abbey's family. The danger to Abbey was too close for comfort. Rohan hated to admit it but Abbey might have been right in not waiting for the police. He lay awake for a long time.

* * *

When Abbey finished her shift the next day, she decided to walk home. The police had come to the hospital and questioned her about the injury to Aunt Sophie and the damage to her car. They'd matched Trevor's footprints and had remanded him in custody, so she felt safe to step out for the exercise. She didn't notice the van parked across the road or the man who watched her from behind his newspaper.

Rohan had suggested he'd run her home when she rang him but Abbey knew he was busy and she needed the exertion to clear her head. At least she'd slept last night, something she hadn't thought achievable with Rohan under her roof.

Aunt Sophie had ended up with a purple eye, a red cheek and a huge black bruise on her bottom, and Abbey felt horribly responsible. If she'd let Rohan stay the first time he'd offered, maybe none of that would have happened.

If anything good had come out of last night's attack, it was that Bella had turned the corner for the better. She'd spoken to Abbey that morning about her plans to get over the experience and they'd shared a weepy ten minutes before Abbey had gone to work.

Bella had decided it was her responsibility to look after her aunt. With surprising meekness, Sophie had accepted her younger niece's ministrations and Abbey wasn't sure if Sophie was sore and sorry or just smart enough to keep Bella busy. Either way, it was another worry off Abbey's mind to see glimpses of her sister's previous calm spirits returning.

Abbey walked down into the town, past the medical centre where Rohan was, and she resisted the impulse to drop in and see what he was doing. Then she passed the spot where she'd first met Kayla. Such a lot had happened in the last two weeks and she knew she'd changed. That change was because of Rohan and she'd have to get used to her new self when he'd gone, but she'd never regret meeting him. How could she?

She'd lived through the last ten years not believing that somewhere there was a man who could make her heart beat faster, her cheeks flush and make the whole world brighter and fresher just because he was in it. Someone who could make her see that she was all woman so she could hold up her head and be proud of her femininity.

She couldn't regret that new knowledge and would always be grateful to Rohan for restoring her faith in men. The heartbreaking thing was that she didn't have the power to give him faith in himself, to show him how much he had to offer and heal him the way he'd healed her.

But maybe that was defeatist. He cared enough to stay on after his time to make sure she and her family were safe. Maybe he was changing, too. He'd said he wasn't cut out for commitment and family but maybe he was more frightened of failing than of the concept. It was a new thought and one that gave her more hope than she'd had before.

As she climbed the hill to her house, she realised that if she didn't have the power to heal Rohan then at least she should try. Because she loved him—she did have a gift to offer. All she had to do was convince him to take it. Maybe, by some miracle, it would help him see how much she thought he was worthy of her love. Maybe she could convince him that she was right for him.

When she unlocked the front door, all was quiet. Abbey poked her head around Aunt Sophie's door but her aunt was asleep in the lounge chair and the TV was off.

She crept up the stairs and no sounds came from the girls' rooms except for the faint drone of a radio.

Bella was asleep, too, and Abbey smiled at the opportunity to have a little more time to herself. Which made her think for a minute—she really couldn't remember when she'd last worried how much personal time she'd had. She had changed.

Her mobile phone rang as she sat on the bed, and she answered it before anyone else could hear it.

'Abbey?' It was Rohan, and she dropped her bag with a little thud.

The relief in his voice was easy to hear. 'Is everything all right?'

She kicked off her shoes. 'Of course it is. I've just walked in. Everyone is asleep here and I've even got time to myself. In fact, I was about to ring you.'

Rohan's voice was dry. 'To tell me that you walked home when I asked you to ring me?'

Abbey pulled the band from her hair and massaged her head one-handed. She couldn't help the smile in her voice. 'No, actually. I was going to ring you to ask you to bring me something home when you come.'

'I should be there about six. We're backed up a bit here. What would you like me to bring?'

Abbey lay back on the bed and her smile broadened. She needed to keep him off balance. 'Champagne and strawberries.' There was silence on the other end of the phone and she tried to picture the expression on his face.

She didn't expect his answer. 'I have the front door key. I may be home earlier than I thought.' Then he hung up.

Abbey put her hand on her stomach because suddenly it was churning with nerves. She rolled over and put her hand to her mouth and wondered if she'd started something she would regret. But her smile was still there and she pushed herself off the bed and grabbed some fresh underwear. A shower suddenly seemed a good idea and she had no idea how much time she had.

Less than ten minutes later Rohan knocked quietly on Abbey's bedroom door. When she didn't answer, he pushed it open and peered into the room. He could hear her in the adjoining bathroom. She had a terrible singing voice that made him grin with delight.

He couldn't stay, but for the moment he placed the unopened champagne and strawberries on her dressing-table and settled himself in the chair to wait.

He had no idea what had come over her but, more than anything, he desperately needed to see her happy. And she'd sounded that way on the phone—

so much so that he'd invented a house call and promised to return to work in half an hour. He just hoped she didn't take too long in the shower because he was going crazy, imagining her routine.

The door opened and Abbey stepped out in a cloud of steam. Her voluptuous breasts were only just contained in an apricot underwired bra and the high-cut matching bikini briefs made her glorious legs stretch for ever. He couldn't think of anything more beautiful to leave work for. But she was going to kill him. He cupped his hands over his eyes to semi-block the vision and coughed.

She shrieked and dashed back into the bathroom and he bit his lip to stop from laughing out loud. Time to leave while the going was good.

'I just dropped in your order, madam, but I have to go back to work now. See you at six.'

When the door shut behind him, Abbey slunk out. That hadn't gone quite to plan. Round one to Rohan. So much for keeping him off balance, but she wasn't giving up.

The house returned to normal not much later. She could hear Sophia Abigail roar with displeasure at the tardiness of her next meal and the sound of Aunt Sophie's next race drifted up the stairs. She sighed and then smiled. Life was pretty good, really. Rohan would be back at six.

Bella even smiled as Abbey passed her on the way to the kitchen. 'Aunt Sophie says she feels much improved this afternoon,' Bella said. Abbey bit her lip.

Obviously Sophie had taken as much tender loving care from Bella as she could handle.

'Thank you, Bella. How are you?'

Her younger sister grimaced and then shook her head. 'I'm OK, Abbey. I look at Vivie and I know I couldn't be that strong. So I'll learn from the experience. But I'll be glad when they catch him.'

Abbey hugged her sister and blinked the tears from her eyes before Bella could see them. 'Me, too. The sooner the better. I should start dinner because Rohan will be here in an hour or so.'

'You like him, don't you?' Bella was thinking about someone other than herself and Abbey knew she was on the mend.

'Too much. But that's OK. I'd rather feel it than be numb.' Afraid she'd given too much away, Abbey hurried off to the kitchen before her sister could say anything.

Dinner turned out to be almost as much fun as the night before Bella's tragic arrival. They all laughed and there was a special shine to Abbey and Rohan that rubbed off on the rest of the party.

When they left to go to the study, Sophie winked at Vivie and Kayla, and Bella huddled in to catch up on the gossip she'd been missing out on.

Oblivious, Rohan and Abbey carried the champagne and strawberries into the study and shut the door. Even Clive was left on the outside and the pop of the champagne cork made those in the kitchen smile.

'So, why did you feel like champagne?'

Abbey shrugged over the top of her glass and Rohan resisted the urge to kiss the answer out of her because he really didn't think he'd be able to stop at a kiss.

He tried again. 'What happened today to turn you into a party animal?'

Her lips twitched and then she gave him the full Abbey Wilson smile and he felt the breath catch in his chest. He almost missed her answer he was that blown away.

'You said that when *the* man comes along, the one who can promise me the stars, I should be ready for him.'

She sidled across the lounge until her hip was firmly and warmly up against his and then she threw one long brown limb over his in an embrace he'd fantasised about. His mouth froze on the rim of the glass and when he could breathe again he sucked in a breath and accidentally inhaled his wine. To his disgust, Rohan spent the next five minutes fighting for air.

When he'd recovered from the aspiration of champagne Abbey had lost momentum and he could tell she was mortified. He'd been like a clumsy teenager. She'd slid back away from him and her hands were clenched in her lap.

'I'm not very good at this,' she said, and he shook his head ruefully. He hated the thought that she was embarrassed by trying to seduce him.

'Abbey Wilson, you have no idea just how good you are at it. Don't you dare apologise for one of two

memories I will take to my deathbed.' He grinned at
her and pushed himself up against where she huddled
at the end of the chaise longue until they were sitting
hip to hip again and her warmth seeped into him.

'The other memory I have is in Technicolor. Glorious apricot. I am never going to forget the vision in
the bathroom mist.' He slid his arm around her and
gathered her close. 'Your offer is so typically generous, Abbey. Thank you, but I don't deserve it and I
won't take advantage of you.' But he had to kiss her.
She kissed him back and all the love and gratitude
and sorrow and heartache of loving for the time
they'd had together and the time that he'd just refused
was in that kiss.

When they drew apart, Abbey wiped the tears from
her eyes because, in effect, he'd said, no, thank you
and goodbye.

'I'd better go to bed, then.'

He stood up and reached down to help her. 'I think
so.'

Rohan lay awake for a long time after Abbey went
upstairs. The others in the kitchen had trooped off a
short while later and the house was silent. His bed
was more comfortable tonight because Abbey had arranged for a single mattress to be made up for him
on the floor, but he knew he wouldn't sleep.

He'd never met anyone like Abbey and he couldn't
believe he'd knocked back her offer. If he wasn't so
sure that one day she'd regret tying herself to him,

he'd be tempted to pretend that he was good enough for her.

Clive barked once outside and it gave him a good excuse to get up and walk around. He found the torch that Abbey had left for him and unlocked the front door. It was a mild night and a few stars were up. The moon was new and cast little light to compete with the darkness.

There was a van he didn't recognise across the road, and he expected Clive to come and see what he was doing but the dog was nowhere to be seen. Probably still not talking to me, Rohan thought. Clive had lost his spot in Abbey's study.

Rohan shone the torch around the yard and towards the garage but it all seemed peaceful. He peered around the side of the house just as a strange noise from one of the spikier bushes drew his attention. He crept closer and his hand tightened on his torch and he berated himself for not bringing at least a poker.

His torchlight swept the grass and then Rohan noticed a lighter patch of grey and caramel fur and a trickle of red. Clive.

At first, he thought the dog was dead, but the strange noise had come from Clive as he'd opened his eyes and tried unsuccessfully to rise. Blood dripped from a cut above his eye and the way he wobbled as he attempted to stand made Rohan think of a head injury. 'OK, mate. We need to get back to Abbey.'

Rohan gathered up the dog in his arms and sprinted for the house. Cold fingers of dread raised the hairs

on the back of his neck in case whoever had bludg-
eoned Clive had made for the front door he'd foolishly left unlocked.

The man climbed the stairs swiftly and headed
straight for Abbey's room. His teeth glinted in the
darkness.

The handle turned slowly under his fingers but the
door swung open before he'd completed a full turn
and he pushed it wider to slip into the room. A glow
from the direction of the bathroom illuminated the
empty bed and made him smile, and he stepped across
to wait against the wall. He stood there for several
moments but it was very quiet and he frowned before
he pushed open the door. The bathroom was empty
and he spun around to search the rest of Abbey's
room. She was gone.

Abbey was outside and hadn't even thrown her
dressing-gown over her short pyjamas. Clive's one
bark had sent her down to find Rohan's bed empty
and she'd gone into the kitchen to locate another torch
before she'd headed out the front door.

As she made it to the bottom step, Rohan sprinted
towards her from the side of the house with a dark
bundle in his arms. He pulled up in a spray of gravel,
bumped her arm and hustled her up the steps.

'Ring the police. Someone's hit Clive and they're
either around here somewhere...' he glanced past
Abbey and then met her eyes '...or already in the
house.'

Abbey twisted her head as she hurried up the stairs. 'Is Clive all right?'

'You can check him in a minute. Move.'

They came through the door and skidded to a stop. A man was standing at the bottom of the stairs with a small handgun pointing right at Abbey's chest.

Nausea rose in her throat from revulsion. She should have thought of her ex-fiancé earlier. No wonder he'd seemed familiar. Perhaps, because of the memories, it wasn't so strange that Abbey's brain had hesitated to recognise him. 'Clayton Harrows. It was you at the hotel!'

Clayton leaned against the bottom banister rail and the smug look on his face made Abbey seethe with frustration. 'You didn't know it was me at the pub, did you?' he sneered. 'I've waited a long time to pay you back for sending me away, and tonight's my night.'

Beside her, Rohan moved slowly to lay Clive on the floor, but Clayton's gun swung over to point at Rohan.

'Keep him up there and don't move. Must be pretty heavy, that dog. Shame you're stuck with him. Can't really throw Abbey's precious dog at me, can you?' He grinned evilly.

Abbey felt the fear rise—fear for Rohan, fear for Clive who was lying limply in Rohan's arms and fear for anyone else in the house who might come out to see what was happening. Funnily enough, she didn't have any fear for herself. She was too angry. Livid. That Clayton had abused her sister was so monstrous she had trouble thinking of anything else. The man was evilly insane.

She glared at him. 'You've already done enough damage. Leave before you do something that will have you rot in gaol for the rest of your life.'

'Grown up a bit, haven't you, young Abbey? So's your sister. Both not bad-looking women.' He smiled again at Abbey's obvious disgust. 'Can't leave now that you've seen who I am. Wouldn't be sensible.' He gestured with the gun towards the door. 'Let's go outside and talk about this.' He chuckled at Rohan's predicament with the heavy dog in his arms. 'Bring your friend.'

Outside was further away from her family and that was a bonus for Abbey. The last thing they needed was a hostage situation inside the house with her whole family. But outside would be more dangerous for herself and Rohan unless they managed to get away.

There was nothing lying around that they could use as a weapon or even a shield. All she had was her torch, and Abbey wished she could think of something.

Abbey turned towards the door and as she got to the top step Rohan bumped against her—deliberately—with Clive in his arms and urgently whispered, 'Dive left and run. I'll cover you. Don't stop.'

Abbey stared at him in disbelief. That would leave Rohan's back exposed. The thought of Rohan dead by Clayton's hand was beyond comprehension and her fear accelerated. 'No,' she whispered back. 'Together or not at all.'

'No talking, children.' Clayton had come a lot closer and he kept the gun aimed at Abbey. 'Any tricks and she gets it first.' He pushed Rohan with his foot. 'If you're real good, you can have it first instead of her.'

They all descended the steps and Rohan searched his brain to think of a way of drawing the fire away from Abbey in a way she would agree to. His arms ached with the weight of Clive. If he didn't put this dog down soon, his arms would be useless anyway. Time was running out.

Rohan hit the bottom step and pretended to stumble. He tipped Clive out of his arms without too much of a bump and then pulled Abbey down in front of him so that he fell on top of her and shielded her with his body. He gritted his teeth as he steeled himself for the impact of a bullet.

He'd sacrifice his life to save Abbey with no qualms and in a flash of comprehension he realised his mother hadn't been a fool after all. He'd been the fool, allowing his own guilt to cloud the issue. Finally he understood her reasoning. Loved ones were everything.

There was no doubt he loved Abbey more than his own life and that certainly reeked of commitment. They'd both just have to live through this and maybe he would have the chance to change his views on a life with Abbey. Now that it might be too late, the picture of being a part of Abbey's family seemed so right, he didn't know why he hadn't seen it before. He loved her and, at this moment, he regretted his fear of commitment. If they lived through this, he wouldn't hesitate again.

When Rohan pushed her to the ground, Abbey knew what he was doing. She twisted under him and her brain was screaming, Don't do this, as the breath was knocked out of her by the weight of his body.

Clayton stood on the bottom step and waved the gun at them. 'Get up now, or I'll shoot you both in the back.' The screech of one of the upstairs windows drew his attention and he twisted his neck to look up.

Before he could alter the aim of the gun, Bella leaned out of the window and without hesitation dropped a large orange plant pot. It made a whistling sound and seemed to sail in slow motion. Bizarrely, the leaves of the shiny green plant waved merrily on the way down. The terracotta base struck Clayton on the side of the head and he hit the ground not long after the pot exploded in front of him.

For Abbey and Rohan the noise sounded like gunfire and tiny pieces of terracotta and potting mix sprayed all over them. The looks they gave each other were full of regrets of opportunities lost and what should have been a magical life together.

'Did I kill him?' Bella's voice drifted down from the window and Abbey blinked. She moved her arms and then her legs and rolled out from under Rohan to meet his bemused eyes. They both turned to look at Clayton's body on the ground and then at an unrepentant Bella who was hanging out of the upstairs window.

'Guess we're not dead.' Abbey's voice shook and she bit her lip at the closeness of their escape.

Rohan glanced skyward for a second in celestial thanks and then looked back at Abbey. 'Guess I get a second chance.' Rohan leaned over and kissed Abbey as if there were still no tomorrow.

'Now, I suppose I'd better follow my Hippocratic oath and see if this creep is alive.' He paused. 'Was he the guy who said you were frigid?' Abbey nodded. Rohan kissed her thoroughly. 'Silly bugger.'

He went to move towards Clayton when he had another thought. 'Was he the man who attacked you?' Abbey nodded once more so Rohan kissed her again. 'No hurry, then.' He kissed her yet another time.

Bella pulled shut the window and by the time she'd made it down stairs all the lights were on and Vivie and Kayla had called the police.

CHAPTER TEN

THE police and ambulance had been and gone. Clayton Harrow still lived and would go from the hospital to prison.

The police had already begun proceedings against Clayton because his wife had changed her statement and withdrawn his alibi for Bella's attack. Frightened since she'd married him, she'd finally broken the hold he'd had over her.

When they'd arrived at Abbey's house, it hadn't taken the police officers long to understand what had happened and they'd accepted Bella's drastic action with remarkable aplomb.

When the uproar in the house had quietened and they were all on their way to bed, Rohan determined to grasp the second chance he'd been offered. He managed to separate Abbey's aunt from the others outside her room and delayed her with a hand on her arm.

'Sophie? One moment, please,' he said, and he thought ironically that he'd never imagined himself in this situation.

'What?' The old lady paused and smiled tiredly at him.

Rohan smiled back and her grin widened. He said,

'You asked me once to let you know if my intentions towards Abbey changed.'

Sophie nodded sagely and her eyes gleamed. 'I did, yes.'

Rohan met her bright-eyed look squarely. 'Well, my intentions have changed. And as you're the senior member of the family, I'd like to ask your permission to try and convince Abbey to marry me.'

Sophie snorted tiredly. 'You won't have any opposition from me, whippersnapper, but you're taking on more than Abbey.'

Rohan smiled ruefully. 'I know, but she's worth it.'

'I wish you luck, then.' Sophie couldn't stop the yawn that slipped out. 'Let me know in the morning what she said. I'm going to bed. I'm too old for these shenanigans at night.'

Rohan watched her hobble away to bed and he shook his head. Life with Abbey wouldn't be dull. All he had to do was convince her to take him on.

Clive rested comfortably in front of the fire. The vet had said he'd be fine but had suggested they watch him for the next four hours in case he deteriorated. Abbey crouched in her heavy dressing-gown to check his breathing.

Most of the house lights were out but there was a small glow coming from the study when Rohan joined Abbey and their canine patient.

Abbey looked up at Rohan and her face was serious. 'He seems all right,' she said.

Rohan helped her up. 'Clive will be fine.' Rohan

drew her into his arms and rested his lips against her hair. 'Are you all right?'

'Yes, I'm all right, thanks.' Abbey relaxed for the first time that night.

Rohan hugged her. 'If I hadn't interfered at the Star, you might have found out earlier.'

She pulled back and looked into his face. 'I have a confession. I was glad to leave that night because I'd already had a really bad feeling about staying there. Who knows what might have happened if I'd tried to confront him on my own?'

Rohan shivered and pulled her back against him. 'Don't even talk about it. I'm still reassuring myself you're alive now. I have never been so scared in my life as I was for you tonight.' He smiled softly at her. 'You could ask me for anything at the moment and I'd give it to you.'

Abbey had Rohan just where she'd never dreamed she'd have him, and the opportunity was too good to miss. She needed to know why he felt that he could never settle down. 'Good. You never told me about your childhood. Tell me now.'

Rohan looked at her. Typical. She wanted to know about him when all he wanted to do was revel in the fact that he loved her and might even be worthy of her love.

He sighed. 'I'm not going to get away without telling this story, am I?'

She shook her head and he pulled her down onto the chaise and put his arm around her. 'If that is what you want.' He stared into the coals of the fire and the dancing flames brought back dark memories.

'My mother worked long hours to make ends meet as a barmaid in the country music town of Tamworth.'

Abbey raised her eyebrows. 'That's where the hat comes from!'

He smiled. 'Yes, and I still enjoy country music.'

Abbey winced and he shook a finger at her. 'Don't be a snob. You'll grow to love it.' He touched her lips with his finger. 'Now, don't interrupt again.'

'My mother was a soft touch for those less fortunate than herself and I used to get so frustrated that she allowed herself to be used by those people. Maybe I had a fair amount of childish jealousy because I wanted all of her attention to myself.'

Abbey couldn't help saying, 'That sounds pretty normal to me, especially for a boy who didn't have a father.'

He shrugged uncomfortably. 'I made her life more difficult than I should have. She tried hard to make me happy and I think she felt there was never enough money to give me what she wanted to.

'Don't get me wrong, we had good times too, but I guess when she died I forgot about those and blamed her for leaving me alone. Actually, I blamed myself, because if she hadn't tried to save me she'd still be alive. Then she was gone before I had a chance to give her all the things she deserved. That was my dream. That one day she would never have to work again and I would spoil her like she wanted to spoil me.'

Abbey's voice was soft. 'How old were you when she died?'

Rohan's face was expressionless. 'Fourteen. One of her charity-case friends went to sleep with a burning cigarette and the house burned down. The woman who caused it all managed to get out but my mother wouldn't leave until she'd found me and pushed me out of the upstairs window.' He raised his eyebrows at Abbey. 'I seem to keep being saved by upstairs windows. Anyway, she saved me but never made it herself.'

He squeezed Abbey's shoulder. 'I was so angry that she lost her life because of a woman who shouldn't have even been in our lives, while her son had needed her.'

Abbey squeezed Rohan's hand. 'Your mother must have been a very special woman.'

'She was.' He smiled ruefully. 'But she was gone. When I left the orphanage, I worked my way through med school and carried on with the goals I'd set. The long hours didn't give me time to grieve. But I couldn't settle down. Whenever I became too uncomfortable without a direction in my life, I'd study another specialty or move to another town.'

'Your mother would be very proud of your achievements. And of the selfless way you tried to protect Clive and me earlier. That was above and beyond the call of duty. So you must have more of your mother in you than you think.'

He met her eyes. 'It's taken me a long time to finish growing up. It's taken until I met you, but I am ready to move on in my life.'

Abbey had known it was coming. She'd promised herself she'd let him go when he needed to and she'd known it would be hard—but nothing had prepared her for the loneliness that opened in her heart at the thought of his departure from her life. She bit her lip and tried to smile through the sudden misting in her eyes. 'So, when do you leave?'

He took her face in his hands and wiped away a tear that fell on her cheek. 'I want to move on spiritually, not physically.' He dropped a kiss on her lips because he couldn't help himself. 'Though I was hoping we could get a little physical later.' Abbey frowned at him and he knew she didn't understand.

He grinned and it made Abbey think of the first time she'd seen him with that blinding smile that had pierced her heart the day he'd arrived.

He went on, 'I've finally found the place to leave my hat and that place is with you. If you'll have me! I believe I've found the only woman in the world who could save me from myself—and I might do a bit of saving, too.'

Rohan smiled into her eyes and the love that shone out at her from his face made more tears gather.

Emotion thickened his voice. 'What we have is so rare and so precious I can't believe you're here in my arms and I'm never going to let you go. Marry me, Abbey. Be my wife and the mother of my children if we're blessed to have them. But, whatever you do, remember I will always love you.'

It was all a dream. It had to be. Rohan's love was something she'd never thought she'd have and his commitment had been a fantasy she hadn't even indulged in. Now he was promising to be with her for ever.

Because of what they had surmounted, Abbey believed it would be for always and even that it was ordained. A love she had for so long imagined would never be hers had suddenly appeared as a whole wonderful world on her horizon.

'Yes. Please.' She smiled mistily. 'I can't wait to marry you and spend the rest of my life with you.' She reached across and kissed him. 'I love you,' she whispered, and this time when she slid her leg over his, he pulled her into his arms and his lips met hers without a hitch.

Much later, when they finally drew apart, she snuggled into the warmth of love that surrounded her just like in her dream, but it wasn't enough and she still had her gift. 'Make love to me, Rohan,' she said. 'Please.'

He kissed the top of her head and hugged her to him. Suddenly he was breathless. For the first time in his life, he was nervous about making love. 'I want this to be perfect for you.'

She rested her fingers on his lips. 'Shh. It's not our

first time. I've dreamt of this, and the reality will belong to us.' She stared into his eyes. 'I love you so much—it can't be anything but perfect,' she said, and kissed him. His tension disappeared as he helped her to stand, because what he wanted couldn't be accomplished on this tiny chaise longue.

They stood together and the gentle light turned her into a golden queen in front of him, and he felt like the ruler of the world claiming his prize. Her hair was free and slightly tangled and he finger-combed it gently, like he'd wanted to do so many times, just to feel the strands pass beneath his fingers like red silk. She tilted her head with his movements and the back of his hand caressed her cheek until she rested her face against his hand and he pulled her closer to nuzzle her neck and drink in the scent of her.

He thought of the first time he'd caught the perfume of her orange blossom skin and the way it had affected him then was no different to now.

It was as if he was about to unwrap a gift he'd longed for all his life. A gift he'd never thought he'd hold against his flesh even briefly—let alone for all eternity.

When he slid her dressing-gown from her shoulders it fell in a puddle around her feet with a shiver of air and swoosh of movement that caught his breath in his chest. She stood before him in the pyjamas he'd dreamed of since Sophia Abigail's birth. Long-legged and desirable as she'd been even in the midst of chaos. He smiled at that memory, too.

The tiny buttons of her shirt magically popped open under his fingers one by one until the swelling edges of her breasts were released by the parting. She gazed at him steadily, unafraid, as he ran his smallest finger down that infinitely desirable valley and past her umbilicus. She shuddered under his touch from the sensation of his cool hand on her heated skin, and he smiled and revelled in the satiny feel of her beneath his hand.

When he slid his fingers beneath the waistband of her pyjama shorts to cup the flatness of her stomach, he devoured her with his eyes. She was here and she was his.

'I can't believe I've found you and you love me.'

She smiled a mysterious, womanly smile that stirred a primitive part of him that ached to carry her off to his cave and keep her there.

She whispered, 'You said the right man would come along and promise me the stars. You are that man, Rohan, and I am yours.'

This time she reached up and stroked his shoulders beneath his shirt, and his muscles cupped into her hand with his sudden tension and suddenly some of his power transmitted itself to her. She pushed her hands under the fabric of his shirt over her wrists until his sleeves slid over his biceps and slithered down to his hands and her fingers followed just to feel his skin under her fingertips.

His shirt fell unheeded and Abbey drank in the sight of the well-defined muscles of his chest and arms. She didn't think she'd ever seen a more beautifully erotic man.

'Now you,' he whispered, and he slid her pyjama shirt off her shoulders until she stood bare to the waist before him and the air in the room seemed to paint her senses with wispy draughts and his adoring look left tangible warmth against her skin. His hand brushed her shorts down her legs in one slow sweep and then quickly he stepped out of his boxers until they were both naked. He took her hand.

'Lie with me,' he said, and drew her down. His fingers were warm and strong and she felt the safest she'd ever felt, with her hand in his keeping.

They sank down onto the mattress on the floor where they lay nipple to nipple, breathing in the magic that joined them together and always would.

Finally, his hand slid down to cup her hip and he rolled inexorably on top of her. The length of him leaned over her and he stared at her with such yearning that she pulled his face down to hers and kissed him until they both ran out of breath.

When the kiss ended, Rohan lifted his head and to him Abbey's face was like that of an angel in the dim light. He smoothed one red tendril of hair from her cheek and the softness under his fingertips was like velvet. His heart seemed to swell in his chest and suddenly he was terrified by how close they'd come to never having this opportunity if things had turned out differently this day. The agony of that thoug' pierced his soul and stung his eyes.

'My God.' The words were torn from him in a ragged whisper. 'If anything had happened to you tonight I would have been glad to go, too. I said I would never lay myself open for this pain but one minute of being with you, one chance to kiss your lips, one taste and smell of your glorious skin, is better than a hundred years alive without you.'

He cupped her face with his hands and there was an urgency and need that his lips communicated to her so powerfully it shook her. Abbey clutched him to her and knew that if she didn't feel him in her soon then she would cry or die or fracture into a million pieces because her heart felt as if it was being torn from her chest by her need for him.

He smiled as if aware of her dilemma and kissed her mouth one last time before his lips moved down to caress her neck and then the undersides of her breasts. Heat spiralled upwards and tortured the rosy peaks of her breasts with frustration. She groaned and sank her fingers into his hair as he circled closer to his target with hot kisses and tiny tastes of the abundance she offered. His other hand crept up and rounded her into an inviting peak and still he didn't swoop. She arched against him, wordlessly entreating him to ease the exquisite agony of the engorgement he'd caused, until he took pity on her.

From there the tempo increased until Abbey swirled into a mindless, grasping, shifting inferno of sensations. In a brief moment of clarity, a fleeting calm in the very eye of the storm, Rohan was poised above her and their eyes met in one long, wordless communication. Then, deliberately, intimately, they were joined as one.

Her breath caught in her throat as he sank into her, each slow plunge of movement driving her closer to orgasm in a way that nothing else could have. More rapidly she surged to meet him and tiny murmurs and breathless moans escaped them both until he was all around her yet lost in her and they merged in a shuddering rush of heat. The magnitude of the sensations made her cling to him, and he to her, until they were once again mortal, and breathless, and pliant against each other with release.

They rested and even dozed in front of the fire, until Rohan opened his eyes and stared at the ceiling in wonder from the discovery of something he'd never realised existed. He turned towards the woman he loved and her eyes were closed. Her skin was flushed and a surge of love made his senses glow with alertness. Bizarrely, some sixth sense warned him that someone was watching him. Rohan twisted his head. Clive's yellow eyes were alert and unblinking as he watched the man with his mistress.

Rohan stared back and Clive held his gaze easily until Rohan's eyes began to water. He blinked, beaten by a dog, and began to shake with the effort of holding in his laughter.

Abbey woke and twisted her head from where she'd been resting on his chest, and looked at his face. 'Are you laughing?'

Rohan grinned and inclined his head towards Clive. 'We've just made love in front of our child.'

Abbey shrugged. 'There's a lot of people in this house—we really should do this sort of thing in my bedroom.'

He smiled at his awesome Abbey and kissed her brow. 'I've been thinking about that. After we're married, I wonder if you'd consider a house of our own?'

Abbey tilted her head. She felt like her whole skin was dotted with those stars he'd promised her and she would have pledged Rohan anything because she knew her place was by his side for ever. 'Where would we live?'

Mischief glinted from his eyes and then darkened as he hugged her. 'I was thinking about next door. There's another old boarding house next door—we could renovate and Bella could stay here with the girls. I love your family but have the feeling it could get crowded.'

Abbey twinkled up at him. 'And what about Aunt Sophie?'

Rohan stifled a laugh. 'It just wouldn't be the same without Sophie. She's lucky. She gets a choice to stay or come with us.'

CHAPTER ELEVEN

ABBEY and Rohan chose to have their wedding ceremony just before sunset at Trial Bay. The bride wore her mother's wedding gown and the gentle breeze teased the tiny train into perfect alignment as if an angel's fingers placed it there with love.

The wedding party assembled on the headland above the beach, and the white sand stretched away in a half-moon around the azure waters of the bay as the minister welcomed the guests.

Behind the congregation, the pink granite walls of the ruins soared in church-like splendour as the minister spoke the familiar words and smiled at the wedding party. The funny old lady was obviously in her element as she gave away the bride and the bridesmaid looked incredibly beautiful—but his eyes kept returning to the couple before him.

The man was tall and handsome in his black suit but it was the look of pure adoration in his face as he made his vows to the bride beside him that touched the minister.

Abbey and Rohan gazed into each other's eyes and pledged their troth as the sinking sun cast a golden ray of light which bathed the couple in blessing for all the years to come. On the other side of the bay, the Norfolk Island pines at South West Rocks pointed long fingers into the sky as if to catch the huge orange ball of the sun as it disappeared from sight.

When Abbey and Rohan turned to their friends and family as husband and wife, a rousing cheer scattered the seagulls that had landed to watch.

Doris waited in regal splendour for the bride and groom with her black duco polished to reflect the occasion, and a white silk ribbon fluttered gaily from her grille to the windshield.

Rohan handed his bride onto the running board and then into the rear seat, where he arranged her mother's wedding gown so seriously that Abbey laughed and beckoned him to join her.

As the car left, they both turned to look back at Trial Bay in the fading light and Rohan covered his wife's hand with both of his. He smiled and the love light in his eyes held their future as it stretched out before them.

'We'll bring our children here in the holidays and camp on the beach, and barbeque the fish we catch. And when the children are asleep, we'll make love in our tent with the sound of waves in the distance.' He smiled at Abbey. 'Did I mention I've never actually been camping?'

She shifted her hip along the seat and her eyes sparkled with mischief as she kissed her husband. 'We'll make sure we have the most comfortable camping mattress I can find.'

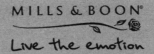

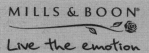

FREE
4 BOOKS
AND A SURPRISE GIFT!

We would like to take this opportunity to thank you for reading this Mills & Boon® book offering you the chance to take FOUR more specially selected titles from the Medical Romance series absolutely FREE! We're also making this offer to introduce you to the benefits the Reader Service™—

- ★ FREE home delivery
- ★ FREE monthly Newsletter
- ★ FREE gifts and competitions
- ★ Exclusive Reader Service discount
- ★ Books available before they're in the shops

Accepting these FREE books and gift places you under no obligation to buy; you may cance at any time, even after receiving your free shipment. Simply complete your details below an return the entire page to the address below. **You don't even need a stamp!**

YES! Please send me 4 free Medical Romance books and a surprise gift. I understand th unless you hear from me, I will receive 6 superb new titles every month for just £2. each, postage and packing free. I am under no obligation to purchase any books and may can my subscription at any time. The free books and gift will be mine to keep in any case.

M3ZE

Ms/Mrs/Miss/Mr ....Initials ....

BLOCK CAPITALS PL

Surname ....

Address ....

....

....Postcode ....

Send this whole page to:
UK: FREEPOST CN81, Croydon, CR9 3WZ
EIRE: PO Box 4546, Kilcock, County Kildare (stamp required)

Offer valid in UK and Eire only and not available to current Reader Service subscribers to this series. We reserve the right refuse an application and applicants must be aged 18 years or over. Only one application per household. Terms and pr subject to change without notice. Offer expires 31st December 2003. As a result of this application, you may receive offers fr Harlequin Mills & Boon and other carefully selected companies. If you would prefer not to share in this opportunity please writ The Data Manager at the address above.

Mills & Boon® is a registered trademark owned by Harlequin Mills & Boon Limited.
Medical Romance™ is being used as a trademark.